So You Want to Be a Superinvestor?

Learn How to Invest Like the Best!

Ashray Jha

Copyright © 2023 Ashray Jha
All rights reserved
First Edition

Fulton Books
Meadville, PA

Published by Fulton Books 2023

ISBN 979-8-88731-732-8 (paperback)
ISBN 979-8-88731-733-5 (digital)

Printed in the United States of America

To my sister Shalini Jha, who was the inspiration behind me writing this book, and I learned from her to always have a smile on my face no matter what struggles I face.

To my grandparents—Pandit Asharfi Jha, Sundari Jha, Dr. Vivekanand Jha, and Shanti Jha—who always wanted all of their kids and grandkids to be happy and successful in all of their endeavors.

To my grandfather Dr. Vivekanand Jha, who encouraged me after my surgery and predicted I would follow in his footsteps and write a book.

To Dr. Bodh Narayan Das and Usha Das, whom I also call Nana and Nani, they both have been by my side and supported me and my family throughout all the difficulties and hardships I faced in life.

To my dad, Himanshu Jha, and my mom, Abha Jha, who have guided and supported me throughout my life. They both refused to give up on me and were always there for me, helping me through all my physical and emotional challenges.

To my cousins Abhinayak Mishra and Jyotsna Jha and my mentor Mike Ranieri, who gave me guidance and support all throughout writing this book.

CONTENTS

Preface: You Can Always Help Others! vii
Introduction: You Should Not Skip This Introduction! xiii

Part 1: Journey into Learning from the Greats! 1
    Chapter 1: You Need to Reevaluate What You
        Learned in the Past! 3
    Chapter 2: You Need to Understand the Early
        Influences on Warren Buffett! 16
Part 2: Demystifying the Stock Market 25
    Chapter 3: You Can Understand the Stock Market! 27
    Chapter 4: You Need to Start Now! 43
Part 3: Understanding the Compounding Machine 47
    Chapter 5: You Just Need to Compound Money! 49
    Chapter 6: You Can Choose the Best Asset Class! 54
    Chapter 7: You Need a Process! 80
    Chapter 8: You Need to Do the Research! 116
Part 4: Buying, Holding, and Selling Stock 121
    Chapter 9: You Need to Have Patience in the Market! 123
    Chapter 10: You Need to Stay with Your Investing
        Journey! 127
    Chapter 11: You Should Not Be Quick to Sell! 141
Part 5: Closing Remarks 143
    Chapter 12: You Can Learn a Lot from Key Mistakes 145
    Chapter 13: You Can Put It All Together 149

Appendix 1: Tables 151
Appendix 2: Sources 173

PREFACE
You Can Always Help Others!

Before I start this book, I want to share some details of my life story with you. In my life, I have faced so many challenges and gone through many hardships. Through hard work and determination, I was able to overcome these obstacles. No matter what obstacle you face in life, I hope my story can inspire you to never give up and tackle your own challenges head-on. I want everyone to have the opportunity to better their lifestyle.

To start my story, I will begin with how my sister was an instrumental part of my life. I had an older sister, Shalini Jha, who was diagnosed with Rett syndrome. Rett syndrome is a rare genetic disorder that affects the neurodevelopment in children. This disease is rare and primarily affects girls. As an infant, those affected develop normally and then gradually begin to lose their motor functions and speech. There are treatments to manage the symptoms, but there is no cure.

When I was younger, I asked my mom what happened to my sister and why my sister was in her condition. My mom explained to me that my sister had Rett syndrome and there was no cure. I could see the pain in my mother's eyes, and I wanted to help. I wanted to be a scientist when I grew up, to find a cure for Rett syndrome and make sure no one else had to go through this pain.

While growing up, I used to watch *Power Rangers*, and I was always air-punching the bad guys when they had a scene on TV. When I was four years old, my mom signed me up for karate. I really enjoyed the activity, and I went on to get my black belt by the age of nine. I grew up during the '90s era when the Chicago Bulls and Michael Jordan won six championships. I wanted to be just like Mike, so I would be playing basketball for hours every day in my driveway. My rule was I need to make one hundred shots before I can go in, unless it started raining.

Everything changed for me when I was ten. I had brain surgery to remove a benign brain tumor from my cerebellum, which affected my balance and coordination. After the surgery, I had lost all my motor functions and had to relearn everything from walking, talking, writing, and typing. I was in a wheelchair after my surgery. My hands shook so much that I could not even wheel my own wheelchair. I was totally dependent on someone else to help me navigate. More than the physical issues, going from being an avid athlete to struggling to move was a major setback for me emotionally. My parents were always there to encourage me and lift my spirits when I was ready to give up. I had to go to physical therapy to regain some motor functions. Some therapists gave up on me, saying that I "plateaued." Thankfully my mom and dad did not listen to these therapists and found me a great physical therapist named Dennise Paule, who never gave up on me. Every Friday and Saturday, Dennise would spend hours working with me on exercises to rebuild my muscle mass and tone. In the summer, Dennise and I would spend long hours three days a week in PT, working on various exercises. In school when I had a free period, instead of goofing off with other kids, I would have to go to occupational or speech therapy just to relearn how to write and speak. I went through a lot of emotional trauma being different from everyone else, but a few members of my family stepped up and supported me.

School was a struggle for me as I couldn't take my own notes and had to dictate everything to an aide. When it came time to doing homework, writing and reading would take me twice as long as everyone else, and sometimes I would be up until 1:00 a.m. just trying to finish my work. What made things worse was some of the teachers did not want me in their honors classes and tried everything in their power to break my spirit. Fortunately, I had two phenomenal teachers, my math teacher, Mrs. Cisnero, and my chemistry teacher,

Mrs. Krupinski, who would work with me every week before or after school to make sure I had the proper notes and understood the material. Both my parents were always taking me early or picking me up from school late so I could meet with my teachers to get extra help. My parents were determined to help me excel in school. More than teachers, Mrs. Cisnero and Mrs. Krupinski were life coaches. Mrs. Cisnero would always motivate me and build up my confidence since others always tried to shatter my confidence. Mrs. Krupinski wanted me to become independent as when I would go to college or start working, I would not have an aide and I would need to take my own notes. She wanted me to get comfortable using a laptop and made me take typing electives to learn how to type. Now, I am very comfortable with typing and using a computer for work.

When I got to college, initially it was great, I made a few close friends that I still talk to today. With all my challenges and managing my day-to-day exercise routines, living independently while studying biomedical engineering in college was very difficult. I worked hard and struggled everyday just to get by. I had multiple knee injuries during my time in college. I had some very good friends who would walk with me to get to my classes. My mom would come almost every other day to help me walk from one end to the other end of campus and then take me to physical therapy sessions. Whenever I had free time, my mom would find any open space on campus and help me with my at-home exercises. Just working on my physical health and lifestyle for most of the day made it increasingly difficult to keep up with my engineering classes, and I wanted to quit every day. Thankfully my parents and aunt Abha Malik would call me every week to keep me on track and not drop out of school. After one of my tests, I got a 50 because I answered the questions correctly, but when it came to drawing the solution, I was unable to draw legibly. My advisor called me into his office and told me if I can't draw, I would never be successful in engineering. I went back to my room and felt hopeless. I already wanted to give up and his statement was no help.

Luck would have it, that in the next semester, my professor for circuits lab, Joe Jesson, happened to work for GE and now ran his own startup. He was just helping out the main professor who taught the course but could not oversee the lab assignments. Joe told the class about all his other projects. After class, Joe and I began talking about his startup and the projects he was working on. Joe said to me, "You seem like a very smart kid, and I need help with one of the pharmaceutical projects I am working on. Do you want to help?"

Thrilled that someone believed in me and wanted me to do work for them, I agreed. I worked every day after class and all night on this project. I enjoyed this work so much and was successful managing the business applications, working on improving the technology, and working on developing the business that I started believing in myself again and wanted to work in finance.

Later that year, my sister passed away. This really impacted my family. We were all taken by shock when this happened. In the last few days, my sister completely stopped eating. Her body was beginning to completely shut down. She held on until I left the house to go back to college and shortly after she had passed. It was extremely heart-wrenching to come back and do all the funeral arrangements. I will never forget the day of the funeral when our lives changed. It is so hard to get used to someone that is a big part of your life, to not be there all of a sudden.

In the summer before my junior year, my dad took me to a networking event at Citigroup, and shortly after I was offered an internship at Citigroup. I worked in the Residential Mortgages Technology group, and I really enjoyed and exceled in that role. I realized I am good at this type of work and that this should be my future career path.

I eventually did graduate engineering college, and I wanted to pursue finance. To help me break into finance for a full-time career, my dad enrolled me into an investment banking class. I completed the class. On the last day, the teacher talked to me and said, "Why are you here? You will never make it in finance. You don't have the look."

At this point, I had so many people doubt and judge me that it was comical. I just laughed and replied, "Watch!" Yes, it was a struggle to get a job for nine months, but one company, Fidelity Investments, decided to take a chance on me. I told the HR managers and the senior leaders my story, and they were willing to accommodate me and knew I would succeed in the job because of my dedication and perseverance. I was enlightened to get a full-time job. I have been working at Fidelity Investments for seven years now, and I am living on my own in an apartment in Jersey City. I wanted to give back, and now I am leading the Enable employee resource group at work, and my goal is to bring awareness to all kinds of disabilities and disabilities in the workplace. Many people are impacted by disabilities directly or indirectly as caregivers, and I want to help others find their voice.

I had a lot of people look down on me, but a lot of other people helped me and took a chance on me. This support helped me succeed in life, and that changed everything. I began to think what is needed that can be used to help people that I am capable of doing? I can share my knowledge and experiences and try to help many people.

I am in no position to give any advice, but I have been investing for myself for many years, and I want to share my knowledge, experiences, lessons learned over the years, and new approaches that enhanced my skill set. I want to help you and many others to succeed in achieving or getting closer to any financial goals you may have. This is why I wrote this book.

INTRODUCTION
You Should Not Skip This Introduction!

Ever since I was very young, around four or five years old, my dad would come home after work and watch the nightly business news. My dad and I would watch *Supermarket Sweep* right after the nightly business news. I was very excited to watch *Supermarket Sweep*, and most of the time I would watch the second half of the news with my dad while I waited for *Supermarket Sweep* to start. In the nightly business news, there would always be two news anchors who would give a rundown of the news and then list all the popular stocks with their price movements. Most of the concepts discussed went over my head.

My dad did explain to me what a stock was. He had an example where a company had been divided into one hundred parts represented with pieces of paper. A company needs money to stay in operation and have money to make investments relevant to the business. In the example, the company needed money for their processes, so it sold each piece of paper to the public for $1. If I had $10, I could buy ten pieces of paper from the company. My dad had $20, so he bought twenty pieces of paper. The founder of the company spent $50 to buy fifty pieces of paper. Other people decided to buy the remaining parts of the company. In exchange for us buying the pieces of paper from the company, we are able to share the profits that company makes. The pieces of paper are not just any ordinary pieces of paper, they represent how many shares of the company you own. Let's say the company makes $200, and that is distributed evenly among the one hundred pieces of paper. Now each piece of paper is worth $2. My dad then asks me how much is my stack of paper worth now?

I look down at my stack of ten pieces of paper, and I begin counting 2, 4, 6, 8 until I get to 20. I exclaimed, "Wow! I paid $10, and now I have $20."

My dad replied, "Yes, but this is just an example to show you how stocks work. There are a few companies that can double your money like in the example. Most of the time a decent company can turn your initial $10 to $12 or $13. Other times that initial $10 investment may become $8."

I liked the idea that stocks could increase my money; however, I was horrified at the thought I could lose money also. The key is to be able to find these wonderful companies that can increase your money for a long period of time. There are thousands of companies with stocks you can choose from, so making investments in stocks can seem overwhelming at first. You might lose money at any given time, but good companies usually bounce back and increase your money over time. Thus began my journey of looking at companies to find the "perfect" stock. Now no stock can be completely perfect, but with proper research, you can make an educated evaluation on which companies offer stocks that are truly wonderful and are as close to "perfect" as possible. Now, I want to share with you what I have learned and help you with your own investing journey.

It was back in the mid-2000s, and my parents and I were sitting around the TV before I had to go to school. An iPod commercial with people line dancing came on the TV. The ad was so interesting, and it looked like everyone was having a blast. I saw the pocket-size device that held over one thousand songs, and I thought that was way better than when I used to carry a bulky Walkman around. Mostly I just liked one song I heard on the radio, but if I wanted to listen to the song whenever I wanted, I had no choice but to buy the whole CD. Now I can just buy an individual song from the iTunes store that I like and have the song stored on my iPod. The old way was so painful that I found it easier to stop listening to music for the most part. Maybe the iPod would force me to listen to music again.

SO YOU WANT TO BE A SUPERINVESTOR?

I exclaimed, "Oh, I want that!"

Immediately my mom said, "Why? You don't even listen to music that much. You have hundreds of CDs, and there are cases in the basement collecting dust. You don't even listen to music anymore."

I thought to myself okay, one parent said no, let me see if the other parent says yes to buying me an iPod.

Knowing that my dad had more of a business approach, I figured maybe I can talk up the company and work my way down to getting an iPod. I then turned to my dad and said, "Remember when I was younger, you told me I can buy whole or parts of a company?"

He replied yes.

Then I said, "Well, I want to buy parts of the company Apple. I think they will change the world, and everyone in that commercial looks so happy. Everyone will want an iPod."

To this, my dad said, "Do you have money? Do you know how much the company costs?"

I shrugged and said no. That was the end of that conversation. Great, now I actually wanted Apple's stock over an iPod.

Fast forward to eighth grade when I was first introduced to the stock market game. If you have never heard of the stock market game, it is a game where each team has a hypothetical $100,000 to construct a portfolio. Daily, the groups record the portfolio performance, and at the end of the month, the team with the most money wins the game.

Our teacher divided the class of thirty into six teams. Each team was in charge of managing a hypothetical $100,000 portfolio. When our team had to select a team lead to make decisions, I told my group about my conviction in Apple and my plan would be to put $100,000 in Apple and then do nothing. None of the other members in the group liked this idea, and I was not selected to lead the group. They thought not taking any action during the unit was a guaranteed way to lose the game. I disagreed with the decision. I figured I eat lunch the period before with everyone in the group, so I was not going to make a big deal about not leading as I didn't want to get kicked out of the lunch group. Again my idea for buying Apple's stock was shut down. However, the team lead that was selected liked what I said and decided to put $10,000 into Apple.

I talked with the team lead, and we discussed why he liked Apple too but would only put in $10,000 in Apple's stock for our portfolio. He explained to me the concept of single stock risk and how diversification works to spread out risk. If something were to happen specifically to Apple and we had $100,000 in the stock, we would not be able to recover. If we put $10,000 into Apple and something bad happens to the stock, we can rely on the other $90,000 to be fine. At the time, this made sense to me. You do not want to put all of your eggs in one basket.

In the following chapters, I will show you why diversification is not the best strategy and is not used by many prominent investors. The team lead also mentioned to me that he started watching business news programs on CNBC when we began this section, and he heard a lot of good things about Apple's future pipeline of products. I nodded, but I only knew of one product, the iPod. I had to do my own research on Apple's pipeline of products. I asked my friend how was he going about doing his stock research. He mentioned he would watch CNBC and the analysts that were on TV provided in-depth stock analysis. After I got home from school that day, I started watching CNBC programs at least two to three times a week. I heard many analysts speak so highly of Apple. They concisely explained what Apple's business does and the future growth potential. Seeing how these analysts were able to look at the future of the company to decide if a stock is worth buying, became a key part of my investing process in the future.

When I started working and had my own investment account, I bought Apple stocks to be a core holding in my portfolio. Finally, no one was telling me that I could not buy Apple. I used the concepts I had learned from my earlier days in school to construct the rest of my portfolio. For years my portfolio coasted along, and I thought nothing of it. I was getting the market average, and I was happy. Then 2020 came, and the coronavirus lockdowns started. I saw my portfolio's value get cut in half. I was left feeling scared, confused, and helpless. The concept of diversification (buying a group of stocks to limit downside risk), which was supposed to protect me, was not working. Was there something wrong with my plan, or should I just keep moving forward? I hated this feeling of helplessness and vowed to never put myself in this position again. Yes, the market will have wild moves from time to time again in the future, but I will have the knowledge to know how to respond in these situations.

This is where my real investing journey begins. Throughout this book, I will share valuable insights and findings from my investing journey. I was using all the academic concepts I learned prior, and now I had one setback. Were the concepts that I was taught in school wrong, or was I just poorly executing the concepts? I started to think about the great investors in the world and how they got to where they are today. All of the greats must have faced many difficult times in the market, but how did they survive? What makes their strategy seemingly better, and can I even use the strategies since I did not have millions of dollars? Time to research!

PART 1

Journey into Learning from the Greats!

CHAPTER 1

You Need to Reevaluate What You Learned in the Past!

When I was in the eighth grade, I played the stock market game in history class as a part of our unit on the stock market. In this unit, our class learned many concepts taught like diversification, efficient market theory, and beta. Once I started working in 2015, I had created my own portfolio by buying shares of Apple stock to be the anchor of my portfolio, since that was my favorite company for a long time. The rest of my portfolio was constructed using methods that I had learned earlier in academia. My portfolio grew at a gradual pace, and I was content with having some extra money. This worked for five years. Then 2020 hit, and there were COVID-19 lockdowns that sent the market into a panic. This was the first bear market that happened to me ever since I was responsible for my own money. My portfolio value was cut in half. Listening to financial news with the constant glum view of how the financial world was about to end made me want to puke. I questioned if anything I learned about the stock market was really relevant. Before I completely abandon investing in the stock market, let me take a step back and think about the best course of action.

I remembered the Mike Tyson retort from one of his fight Q&A sessions, "Everyone's got a plan until they get punched in the mouth" (Berardino 2021). The market just "punched" me in the mouth, and my plan went out the window. Well, the market "hit" me hard but did not knock me out of the investing fight. Now let me find a new plan and "punch" the market back even harder so I can win the investing game.

Initially, I began to spiral in my thoughts and panic. Maybe it was easier to just take out the remaining money that I had in the market and call it quits. Maybe the media was right, and it was the end of the financial world. As I collected myself, I began to think there are so many great investors throughout history that have been successful. These investors have faced so much adversity throughout their careers. If any one of these investors were to quit the first time they faced hardship, we would not be saying they are the greatest at the investing game. I asked myself what was I doing wrong. It was apparent to me that the concepts that were taught in academia were not working for me, but I needed to reevaluate what I had learned. I knew what I learned in school was right as I was able to be successful for a couple of years, but did the academic concepts hold true outside the vacuum in certain situations? I had to understand the difference between diversification and concentration, efficient and inefficient markets, and whether beta is actually risk. Value investor Christopher H. Browne of Tweedy Browne gave a speech at the Graham and Dodd Value Investing Center at Columbia University in November 2000, where he criticized the nonvalue add financial information taught in most schools. "A whole body of academic work formed the foundation upon which generations of students at the country's major business schools were taught [concepts such as] Efficient Market Theory and Beta. In our humble opinion, this was a classic example of garbage in/garbage out" (Browne 2000, p. 1). I have been coding ever since I was in college and learned, no matter how good the query I write is, if I put bad inputs in the code, then I will get bad results out. What helped me in learning how to code was to see what not to do first, and that really helped me understand the right way to code. Let's apply this same methodology to investing and see where improvements can be made! Let's now reevaluate and discuss the six main topics that I learned in school.

SO YOU WANT TO BE A SUPERINVESTOR?

1. Diversification

Most financial advisors preach that you need a well-diversified portfolio to protect yourself from market downturns. Is diversification the best strategy for protection when the market goes down? When the market tumbled in 2020, all the stocks in the S&P 500, Nasdaq, and Dow Jones were negatively affected unless the stock was a pandemic play like Clorox or 3M. If hundreds of companies all had the same ill fate, what did diversification actually do? Diversification clearly did not protect my portfolio from being cut in half in 2020. I started to research this topic in depth, and I came across a study from value investor Joel Greenblatt. In his book *You Can Be a Stock Market Genius*, he shows us how excessive diversification does not help.

Intuitively, you would probably agree that there is an advantage to holding a diversified portfolio so that one or two unfortunate ("bonehead") stock picks do not unduly impair your confidence and pocket. On the other hand, is the correct number of different stocks to own in a "properly" diversified portfolio 50, 100, or 200?

Even if you took the precaution of owning 9,000 stocks you would still be at risk for the up and down movement of the entire market. This risk, known as market risk, would not have been eliminated by your "perfect" diversification.

Statistics say that owning just two stocks eliminates 46% of the non-market risk of owning just one stock. This type of risk is supposedly reduced by 72% with a four-stock portfolio, by 81% with eight stocks, 93% with 16 stocks, 96% with 32 stocks, and 99% with 500 stocks.

1. After purchasing six or eight stocks in different industries, the benefit of adding even more stocks to your portfolio in an effort to decrease risk is small, and
2. Overall market risk will not be eliminated merely by adding more stocks to your portfolio. (Greenblatt 1997, pp. 20–21)

Let's say you own two stocks, and one doubles while the other stock returns 0%. You will earn a 50% total return in your portfolio. Owning two stocks is still very risky, so what if we own four stocks instead? One stock doubles, and the other three stocks are flat. That will only be a 25% total return in your portfolio. From Greenblatt's study, we see that most of the risk is eliminated when you get to sixteen to thirty-two stocks. If you were to own ten stocks, and one doubles while the other stocks are flat, that is a 10% return. If we do the same calculation with twenty stocks, that is a 5% total return. As you can see, the more stocks that you own, you have to be right on more decisions, and there is a minimal decrease in risk after holding about sixteen to thirty-two stocks.

Then I began to look at the portfolios at some of the greatest investors like Warren Buffett and Peter Lynch, who have more than thirty stocks in their portfolio. I started investigating how were they able to build their fortune having thirty or more stocks. This seems like excessive diversification. The answer was hiding in plain sight. Buffett and Lynch both allocated and concentrated their portfolio into a few top holdings to build wealth and then diversified into many more holdings to preserve wealth. According to Stanley Druckenmiller, it is far better to have a concentrated rather than diversified portfolio. "Diversification is the most destructive, overrated concept in our business. Look at George Soros, Carl Icahn, Warren Buffett. What do they have in common? They make huge concentrated investments. You need ruthless discipline. If the reason you invested changes get the hell out and move on" (Diversificationquotes).

Another famed investor Bill Nygren had this to say on diversification: "Diversification is only a free good if one cannot identify mispriced securities. Once the concept of mispricing is introduced, diversifying away from undervalued securities reduces a portfolio's expected return. Instead of more diversification always being better, diversification becomes a trade-off: it lowers the risk but at the cost of also lowering expected return. We don't want to dilute our best ideas any more than is required to be prudent" (Diversificationquotes).

Looking at Buffett's and Lynch's portfolio, it is apparent you can do well with a concentrated portfolio as long as you can capitalize on market inefficiencies. Academics tell us the markets are efficient, but I don't think we can take this at face value. Let's explore this concept further.

2. Inefficient Markets

Many academics believe and teach the efficient market theory. This theory states that all relevant stock information is already accounted for in the stock price. There can never be an undervalued stock. No one can beat the market, and if anyone does, it is by pure luck. If this was true, there would not be investors like Warren Buffet, Charlie Munger, Howard Marks, Bill Ruane, Bill Ackman, or any of the other Superinvestors of Graham and Doddsville that consistently beat the market every year. How are all of these people from the past and hopefully you in the future just plain old "lucky"?

Even if you have never invested money in the stock market, you know that some days the market goes up, and on other days the market goes down. Occasionally the market bubbles and goes up to levels never seen before, and other times the market breaks down and spirals out of control. By saying the market is always efficient and all information is known at all times, the efficient market practitioners are essentially saying that all investors are like ducks floating on top of the water. The investor's portfolio rises when the water rises and sinks as the water comes down. There is nothing the investor can do but to follow the movements of the market. It is useless to even try as you will always get the market returns. Capitalizing on this flawed and predictable thinking is what allowed Warren Buffett to get so rich. "Naturally the disservice done [to] students and gullible investment professionals who have swallowed Efficient Market Hypothesis has been an extraordinary service to us. In any sort of a contest—financial, mental or physical—it's an enormous advantage to have opponents who have been taught that it's useless to even try" (Buffett 1988).

The belief that the market is efficient makes the assumption that all investors know all the information out there and act the same way. This is simply not true. Imagine you and your neighbor are investors. Both of you have the same socioeconomic conditions and access to the Internet to find the same information on a company. Do both of you decide to buy the exact same stocks? Most likely no, because both of you processed the information differently due to different experiences that influenced your decision-making.

Seth Klarman points out, "Despite the comfortable academic consensus of market efficiency, financial markets will never be efficient because markets are, and will always be, driven by human emotions: greed and fear" (*Efficientmarketquotes*).

Peter Lynch famously said, "I also found it difficult to integrate the efficient-market hypothesis (that everything in the stock market is 'known' and prices are always 'rational' with the random-walk hypothesis that the ups and downs of the market are irrational and entirely unpredictable). Already I'd seen enough odd fluctuations to doubt the rational part, and the success of the great [investors that I worked with] was hardly unpredictable. It also was obvious that Wharton professors who believed in quantum analysis and random walk weren't doing nearly as well as my new colleagues, so between theory and practice, I cast my lot with the practitioners. It's very hard to support the popular academic theory that the market is rational when you know somebody who just made a twentyfold profit in Kentucky Fried Chicken, and furthermore who explained in advance why the stock was going to rise. My distrust of theorizers and prognosticators continues to the present day" (*Efficientmarketquotes*).

This brings us to the question, how should you act during the boom and bust periods in the stock market? In a market filled with many people, not everyone will digest news in the same way, and that can lead to inefficient markets. Can your stomach handle a 50% loss without panicking? Your stock might get caught up with the irrational selling in a market panic, but can you shrug off the bad news and hold on to your wonderful stock?

The good news of academics teaching efficient market theory is that it is ingrained in most money managers, and it is easy to predict how they will react in certain situations by either buying or selling stocks en masse, leading to inefficient markets.

3. Beta

In the eighth grade, we learned about the stock market and the concept of beta. This concept measures the volatility of a stock compared to the volatility of the S&P 500. The closer the beta is to 1, the safer the stock is supposed to be. This is great in theory but is only relevant to past performance. There is no way that past movements of a stock compared to the index will be an accurate tool to predict the future volatility and risk for a stock. Prominent value investor Seth Klarman stated in the "Preface" of Benjamin Graham's *Security Analysis*, "Academics and many professional investors have come to define risk in terms of the Greek letter beta, which they use as a measure of past share price volatility: a historically more volatile stock is seen as riskier. But value investors, who are inclined to think about risk as the probability and amount of potential loss, find such reasoning absurd. In fact, a volatile stock may become deeply undervalued, rendering it a very low risk investment" (Klarman 2008). For example, let us say that you are looking to buy a wonderful company's stock that is trading at $100. The S&P 500 is also trading at $100. Due to factors of an irrational market and panic selling, the S&P falls to $80, and the wonderful stock falls to $60. The stock has a higher beta, but the true fundamentals of the company, which has great earnings and produces free cash flow, have not changed. You reason that both the stock and the S&P 500 will return to a $100 price. Would buying the wonderful company stock at $60 actually be risky? According to beta, it is very risky to buy at $60, but I think it is even riskier to ignore the fundamentals of the business.

Seeing the erratic movements of stocks during the steep market decline during the 2020 pandemic, I noticed the lower beta stocks were affected in the same way as higher beta stocks. Granted the percentage loss in most blue-chip low beta stocks was less than some other tech stocks that had a higher beta, but to me, a loss is a loss. In sports, it does not matter if you lose the game by 20 or 2 points because at the end of the day, you lost the game. You have to move on and think in terms of the whole season. You lost the game, but you have to adjust to win the next game. Hopefully your cumulative record will allow you to advance to the playoffs. In investing, beta is not telling me much about winning or losing just the magnitude of potential losses. I wanted to investigate if beta was actually useful.

While doing my research, I came across this quote from Warren Buffett: "In business schools, where volatility is almost universally used as a proxy for risk. Though this pedagogic assumption makes for easy teaching, it is dead wrong: Volatility is far from synonymous with risk. Popular formulas that equate the two terms lead students, investors and CEOs astray" (Buffett 2015). He did not mention beta by name; however, looking at volatility of a stock compared to the volatility of the market is referred to as beta.

In his book *Margin of Safety*, Seth Klarman had this to say about the use of Beta: "I find it preposterous that a single number reflecting past price fluctuations could be thought to completely describe the risk in a security. Beta views risk solely from the perspective of market prices, failing to take into consideration specific business fundamentals or economic developments. The price level is also ignored, as if IBM selling $50 per share would not be a lower-risk investment than the same IBM at $100 per share" (Szramiak 2016). So now I began to wonder, if beta is not risk, then what is the correct way to think about risk?

I found the answer in a quote from Li Lu of Himalaya Capital (a value investment fund). "Till this day, the vast majority of individual investors and institutional investors still follow investment philosophies that are based on 'bad theories.' For example, they believe in the efficient market hypothesis, and therefore believe that the volatility of stock prices is equivalent to real risk, and they place a strong emphasis on volatility when they judge your performance. In my view, the biggest investment risk is not the volatility of prices, but whether you will suffer a permanent loss of capital. Not only is the mere drop in stock prices not risk, but it is an opportunity. Where else do you look for cheap stocks?" (*Efficientmarketquotes*).

All three of these esteemed investors point out the flaws in using beta to determine risk. A better way to look at risk is to determine the probability the investment is to face a permanent loss of capital. Volatility only causes a temporary paper loss and only becomes a permanent loss if you sell at the bottom. Instead, volatility should be welcomed as it is an opportunity to find undervalued or add to stock positions. In his speech "The Superinvestors of Graham and Doddsville," Warren Buffett points out, "One quick example: The Washington Post Company in 1973 was selling for $80 million in the market. At the time, that day, you could have sold the assets to any one of ten buyers for not less than $400 million, probably appreciably more. The company owned the Post, Newsweek, plus several television stations in major markets. Those same properties are worth $2 billion now, so the person who would have paid $400 million would not have been crazy.

"Now, if the stock had declined even further to a price that made the valuation $40 million instead of $80 million, its beta would have been greater. And to people that think beta measures risk, the cheaper price would have made it look riskier. This is truly Alice in Wonderland. I have never been able to figure out why it's riskier to buy $400 million worth of properties for $40 million than $80 million" (Buffett 1984, p. 14).

Later on in the book, I will go into more detail on how to asses investment risk.

4. *Short-Term Performance*

While playing the stock market game, my class also got into the bad habit of looking at the paper every day to track daily stock movements. The class was solely focused on short-term results. Some students would skip lunch to go to the library to use the computer and sell the positions in the portfolio if something went wrong during the half-hour lunch period.

This reminds me of a *Seinfeld* episode where Jerry gets coaxed into buying a stock with his friends. He is told there is no risk as the other big investor will tell him when to sell. The major investor suddenly falls ill and is taken to the hospital. Now Jerry is left to track the investment himself. Every day Jerry looks at the paper to see the stock performance. After three days of the stock declining, Jerry just wants to get out of the stock and sells in haste to save his peace of mind. A few days after he sold, the stock appreciates in value, and Jerry is going crazy again for making a bad decision.

Not wanting to go crazy like Jerry, I set out to find the best way to limit my emotions in investing. What worked best for me was taking a long-term value-oriented approach. Once I started to play with a compound interest calculator, I began to see how a small investment held for many years that grew at an average rate could provide life-changing results. I would be investing for many years to come, so would the daily fluctuations and short-term performance of a stock be of importance to me? I am going to invest for decades not days.

5. *Time Horizon*

Have you ever wondered how did Warren Buffett become so rich? He did not start out with a huge fortune. Buffett bought his first stock when he was eleven years old, and as of 2020, Warren Buffett was worth $84.5 billion. Most of Buffett's fortune was accumulated after his sixtieth birthday. So what is his secret? Essentially it comes down to buying stocks of wonderful companies and holding on to the stock for long periods of time. Buffett has been compounding money at 22% annually for almost seventy years. Initially Buffett started investing small amounts, but over time the smaller investments grew to huge sums of money. Even a small amount of money that is invested for multiple years and compounds at a market average of 8–10% a year can grow to a substantial sum. Now let's change this thought experiment a little: if you spend less time in the market but have higher returns, can you build a fortune better than Buffett?

One day I was reading the *Psychology of Money* by Morgan Housel, and I came across an example showing the importance of time in investing. At the time Housel wrote the book in 2020, hedge fund manager Jim Simons of Renaissance Technologies had compounded money at 66% annually since 1988. Simons has produced returns three times better than Buffett's 22% return; however, Simons has a net worth of $21 billion. How is it possible that Simons has produced three times the annual returns but is not even close to Buffett in terms of net worth?

SO YOU WANT TO BE A SUPERINVESTOR?

"Simons did not find his investment stride until he was 50 years old. He's had less than half as many years to compound (money) as Buffett. If James Simons had earned his 66% annual returns for the 70-year span Buffett has built his wealth he would be worth—please hold your breath—sixty-three quintillion nine hundred quadrillion seven hundred eighty-one trillion seven hundred eighty billion seven hundred forty-eight million one hundred sixty thousand dollars" (Housel 2020, p. 55). It is astonishing to think that Simons is the better investor in terms of annual returns, but due to the time in the market, Buffett is known as the best investor in the world.

Think about planting an apple tree. When I was in the first grade, I bought an apple tree for my mom. It was just a small tree that we placed in our backyard. My mom would water the tree as needed. By the time I was in the second grade, there were no apples on the tree yet. I thought this tree was a dud. I wanted to get rid of the tree and just go to the store and buy an apple pie. I would be happy instantly and would not have to wait even longer for the tree to produce apples just to make fresh apple pie. I gave up on the tree. My mom kept the tree, and after five to seven years, the tree finally started producing apples. Eventually there were so many apples, we could not possibly eat them all. After another six to seven years, the tree had become a majestic beauty. Eventually the tree branches were collapsing under their own weight, and the tree was cut down. Similarly in investing, you may not see spectacular results after a year or two. However, if you remain disciplined and continue investing over a long period of time, your initial sum of money will begin to grow into a really large sum. The more time that is given to compounding an investment, the returns will be even greater. It is also important to realize the various growth stages of a company and when the company has fully matured and can no longer continue to grow. When this happens, it is probably a good time to think about selling or trimming the investment. No matter how big your portfolio becomes, if you don't have the ability to survive in the market, all your efforts are for nothing.

6. *Longevity*

Along with time, one has to have longevity in the market. The stock market will have ups and downs, but if your portfolio has an iron fortress, it can protect your portfolio and prevent you from being forced to give up. How do we protect our investment interests and survive?

In eighth grade, we played the stock market game for no longer than one to two months before moving on to the next lesson. The timeframe was so short that there were barely any market changing events during the course of the lesson. None of the hypothetical portfolios were battle tested for the real world. If any of the stocks in a team's hypothetical portfolio was a meme stock that went up 500% in a month, that team had won the game. In the following month, if that meme stock declared bankruptcy, it would not matter as the game was over. We have seen in the previous section the importance of investing in the market for long periods of time. If we were to hold our carefully selected stocks over many years to enjoy compounding, we would face many market events that could force us out of the market.

How should we look at market changing events if we want to survive in the market? Here are a few keys to surviving in the market:

1. Don't get carried away with debt. I will show you later on in the book how to look at a company's balance sheet to determine if the company has too much debt. Similarly, the individual investor should not use excessive debt or take out large "margin loans" to buy stocks.
2. Don't panic and sell during corrections or recessions.
3. Don't believe there is only one worldview, or each passing trend will change the world forever. There are multiple viewpoints on everything, and it is important to understand all the points to be well-rounded.
4. Don't get frustrated with the lack of immediate results and quit.

SO YOU WANT TO BE A SUPERINVESTOR?

The longer you can survive and stay invested in the market, that is what can make compounding work wonders. Compounding doesn't need huge returns, just good returns sustained for the longest period of time.

Clearly academic theories have a lot of flaws. Are there other strategies out there? If I am going to learn a new strategy, why don't I learn from the best? Everyone has heard of Warren Buffett, but how did he do it? Were his methods so complicated that only he can be the greatest, or are there many disciples that follow his strategies successfully? My goal is to be the best at investing. Maybe I won't be better than Warren Buffett, but he has a lot of disciples (Superinvestors) who are also wildly successful. What is preventing me from joining the ranks of being a Superinvestor? If I become a Superinvestor that is great, but what is better is helping other people reach or get closer to their goals too. This is my motivation behind writing this book, and I hope we all have an opportunity to succeed. The rest of this book will highlight the different approaches that have been used by some of the greatest investors. Nothing in this book should be considered as advice. My goal is for the reader to understand differing viewpoints and make the best decision for themselves.

CHAPTER 2

You Need to Understand the Early Influences on Warren Buffett!

Ben Graham and Mr. Market

The stock market can be a very intimidating place. What is the best way to understand the market? According to Canadian Superinvestor Prem Watsa, "Some of the best early advice I got was to forget all I'd learned in business school about efficient markets and instead read Ben Graham. You either take to it or you don't, and I knew right away that this was how I wanted to do it" (*Efficientmarketquotes*).

Benjamin Graham created the fictional character Mr. Market to illustrate that the stock market is not an intimidating monster. Imagine you are a business owner with a partner, Mr. Market, who wants to buy your share of the business. Everyday Mr. Market visits you and quotes a different price to buy your share of the business. Mr. Market will offer to buy your share of the business at a low or high price depending on his mood that day and not on the business value. It is up to you to decide if you want to keep or sell your portion of the business based on the offer (Graham 2003). Another way to think about this is, let's say you own a house and someone makes an offer to buy your house. If you are not planning on selling your house, no matter how strong or weak the housing market is, you are not likely to sell your house. However, this person is determined to get a house, so he comes back every day and makes an offer that changes based on his mood. What should you do? There is no media outlet that will provide you real-time updates of the price of your home, but you have a good estimate of the value of your home. Knowing the value of your home allows you to make an informed decision on if you want to accept or reject the offer. Similarly, in the stock market, one should ignore the changing real-time ticker prices and only make buy or sell decisions based on the intrinsic value of a stock.

Ben Graham was one of the few people who had a traditional investing approach that was centered on value. His teachings of Mr. Market is timeless; however, some of his theories have changed over time. Graham believed in a "cigar butt" approach. In the cigar butt method, Graham advocates finding stocks that are trading well below the sum of all the company's asset values. Eventually the stock prices will rise back to fair value of all the assets. If the stock price does not go up and the company actually goes into bankruptcy, then you can profit during a liquidation where all assets are sold at the true value. By buying a collection of undervalued stocks regardless of the quality of the company, the investor can get one last "puff" and see the stock rise. This was the foundation that was used by many investors focused on value, specifically Warren Buffet and Berkshire Hathaway. When Charlie Munger came along, he tweaked this methodology for the better.

Charlie Munger and the Shift in Investing

Warren Buffett attended a course taught by Benjamin Graham on investing at Columbia University. The Graham method was to find and buy every single stock that was trading under the sum of all assets, or net current asset value. These undervalued stocks were called "cigar butts" as they were low-quality companies that were trading at a price much lower than their asset value and had one more "puff" left in them. An investor would buy all the undervalued stocks trading in the market and hope for the price to rise. A few stocks would have one last "puff," but most would just be worthless low-quality stocks. The trick was to select more winners than losers for an investor to profit. During Buffett's early career, he sought out advice from a trusted friend Charlie Munger. Munger later joined Berkshire Hathaway in 1978 and explained to Buffett that instead of buying every cheap stock, it is better to focus on higher quality companies that were undervalued. Buffett took this to heart, and by 1989, he said in a letter to shareholders, "It's far better to buy a wonderful company at a fair price than a fair company at a wonderful price" (Buffett 1990). The change to focus on and make large investments in wonderful companies was one of the biggest factors contributing to Buffett's amazing performance.

I wanted to learn more about this wildly successful approach, as I had just scratched the surface and there was a lifetime of learning ahead of me. I read many books trying to explain how the dynamic team at Berkshire Hathaway invested. Each book had bits and pieces of how investment decisions were made at Berkshire Hathaway. Finally, I came across this interview from Charlie Munger with BBC on the criteria used at Berkshire Hathaway to invest in a business:

1. We have to deal in things that we're capable of understanding.
2. Once we're over that filter, we have to have a business with some intrinsic characteristics that give it a durable competitive advantage.
3. Then of course, we would vastly prefer a management in place with a lot of integrity and talent.
4. And finally, no matter how wonderful it is, it's not worth an infinite price. So we have to have a price that makes sense and gives a margin of safety, given the natural vicissitudes of life.

"That's a very simple set of ideas. And the reason our ideas haven't spread faster is they're too simple. The professional classes can't justify their existence if that's all they have to say. It's all so obvious and so simple, what would they have to do with the rest of the semester?" (Charlie Munger, Interview with the BBC, 2015).

If it is easy and I can learn this style of investing in less than one semester, I will just keep doing my research, and in no time I will also become a Superinvestor. Boy was I wrong, because I have now been doing research for more than two years on Berkshire Hathaway strategies and some of the disciples of the Oracle of Omaha. I have understood the four principles Charlie Munger and Warren Buffett use, but I am still finding new information that allow me to have a comprehensive investing strategy. For now, I have gathered a ton of information that I want to share with you so you can also start your investing journey. Investing is a life long journey, and I am learning more things every day while embarking on this quest for knowledge.

In my quest for knowledge, I noticed multiple investors followed or had roots in Benjamin Graham's style of investing but had different yet important experiences and views on life providing them with a slight twist to investing. Some investors were better at explaining market cycles; others explained investor psychology or understanding businesses well that were incorporated into their individual investing philosophy. No matter the twist, all of these investors had their roots based on understanding the fair value of a business that has been used by Benjamin Graham and later Warren Buffett. I figured I would take all the different views and incorporate them all into my investment strategy.

The hardest part for me was part 3 of the Berkshire Hathaway investing strategy to evaluate management. Unless you are a prominent figure in the business community, you do not have access to management of other companies. Since I do not have access to CEOs of companies, how can I judge management? Understanding management is a core component in Buffett and Munger's investing practice. Did I have to abandon this investing strategy before I even started?

I started listening to many investing podcasts. In one of the episodes, an investor mentions he reviews SEC (Securities Exchange Commission) filings specifically all the accounting tables and management's discussion of the financials to evaluate management. I do not have an accounting degree, and initially looking at tables and SEC fillings was very boring. I read many financial accounting books some even three times and went through each line in the tables to understand where the numbers came from in the accounting tables.

Some of the rows were used in calculations that told a bigger story about the company. Learning accounting was like watching paint dry. It was a painful process, but I enjoy the challenge of learning new and useful subjects. Once I understood accounting, going through SEC documents and tables are now fun for me. I will do my best to make sure the accounting in this book is not as painful.

While doing my research, I found a lot of qualitative information on evaluating a business. What I struggled to wrap my head around was how each of these investors determine the intrinsic value of a stock and how they predict the future growth of the stock. After reading numerous books, I was finally able to find the answer. All of these investors had different methods for determining intrinsic value. No one has a surefire way to determine intrinsic value, but it is far better to have a reasonably close than arbitrary sense of true value. I took some other important financial calculations and incorporated these calculations with the various other strategies I learned. I, too, drew on my life experiences to craft my own investing strategy. Later on in this book, I will walk you through how I calculate intrinsic value and apply a margin of safety.

Still the academics did not want to accept that a strategy other than their concepts was working. Instead of trying to understand why Buffett outperformed the market, the academics said that Buffett is just a lucky coin flipper. They claimed a few orangutans flipping coins could have the same results. In 1984, Buffett had a perfectly crafted response.

The Speech Heard around the World: "The Superinvestors of Graham-and-Doddsville"

For the past two years now, I have spent my spare time reading many investing books and articles written about Warren Buffett, Charlie Munger, and Berkshire Hathaway. I learned about Buffett's teacher Benjamin Graham and his "cigar butt" investing approach. Graham taught this traditional investing approach of buying any stock trading under net current asset value. That was later modified by Charlie Munger to focus on wonderful companies trading at a reasonable price. This change in approach led to Berkshire Hathaway becoming the powerhouse it is today. Many academics in the past and even today believe in many of the concepts taught all throughout many schools and that no one can beat the market. Having disbelief that Warren Buffett beat the market for decades, the academics wrote him off as a "lucky coin flipper." If you were to win the lottery, that is extremely lucky, but beating the stock market for almost two decades at the time of the intense criticism from academics does not seem lucky. There must be something special that the academics were missing. I needed to find Buffett's response to being called a "lucky coin flipper."

In 1984, Buffett went back to Columbia Business School where he learned from Benjamin Graham and published his famous article, "The Superinvestors of Graham-and-Doddsville." He delivered one of the most influential speeches that is now the cornerstone of value investing. To prove the academics wrong, Buffett starts by giving an example of a national coin flipping contest.

> Let's assume we get 225 million Americans up tomorrow morning and we ask them all to wager a dollar. All of them call the flip of a coin with the winners gaining a dollar from those who called wrong. Each day the losers drop out, and on the subsequent day the stakes build as all previous winnings are put on the line. After ten flips there will be approximately 220,000 people who have correctly called all the flips with winnings a little over $1,000.
>
> After ten more flips there are 215 people who have successfully called their coin flips and turned one dollar into a little over $1 million. $225 million would have been lost, $225 million would have been won. Unable to explain what has happened, some business school professor will probably be rude enough to bring up the

fact that if 225 million orangutans had engaged in a similar exercise, the results would be much the same—215 egotistical orangutans with 20 straight winning flips.

However Buffett points out one very interesting point about luck, for one thing, if (a) you had taken 225 million orangutans distributed roughly as the US population is, if (b) 215 winners were left after 20 days, and if (c) you found that 40 came from a particular zoo in Omaha, you would be pretty sure you were on to something. You would try to find every commonality and any extraordinary concentrations of success.

He then states,

> You will find that a disproportionate number of successful coin-flippers in the investment world came from a very small intellectual village that could be called Graham-and-Doddsville. All of the successful investors share a common intellectual patriarch, Ben Graham. Each investor has gone to different places and bought and sold different stocks and companies, yet they have had a combined record that simply cannot be explained by random chance. Since each investor is not just copying Ben Graham to a tee, the students have applied the same framework and decided on their own manner of applying the theory to become successful. (Buffett 1984, p.5)

The common intellectual theme of the investors from Graham-and-Doddsville is this: they search for discrepancies between the value of a business and the price of that business in the market. Essentially, they exploit those discrepancies without the efficient market theorist's concern. The Graham and Dodd investors do not discuss beta, the capital asset pricing model, or covariance in returns among securities as there is little use of these topics in value investing. The investors simply focus on two variables: price and value.

This made sense to me, and I wanted to learn from all the successful investors. While looking at the great investors, I found that many exceled in specific areas. Namely Peter Lynch's teachings were crucial for me to understand the macro environment and how this effects stocks. Howard Marks taught me about investing cycles and positioning. Warren Buffett and Charlie Munger taught me about investing and how to identify wonderful businesses. Many others provided key advice and guidance.

I used all of these findings to churn my whole portfolio and focus on value investing principles with my own approach. I had to go through a long process to find a new plan. All of the vital information was scattered across multiple sources. After doing a lot of research, I started putting it all together. My new approach was working for me and allowed me to recover from the massive financial blow suffered in 2020. Now I want to share with you all the vital information on how to evaluate a business and how my life experiences have guided me so far through my investing journey. I hope my experiences, research, and observations can serve as a guide to others to help us all win in this game of investing.

PART 2

Demystifying the Stock Market

CHAPTER 3

You Can Understand the Stock Market!

By now, I had determined that investing based on determining intrinsic value was vastly superior to academic theories. It seemed logical to me that when I go to the store, I determine the value of an item and pay a price that seems reasonable. Why wouldn't this approach work in investing? As I was beginning to embark on this new quest for knowledge, I would watch so many financial programs on TV. I had seen many analysts talk about the markets and use financial jargon that just confused me. I listened to the constant noise on TV and thought there is so much information that I do not know about the stock market that I would never be able to invest. However, there was one game that helped me demystify the stock market.

How Monopoly Taught Me How to Think about the Stock Market

In the early parts of the 2020 pandemic, I began to play Monopoly World Edition online. There are many editions of Monopoly that stem from the original version. In each version, all players have an equal amount of cash and move across the board buying, trading, or selling properties. A player wins the game when all the other players run out of cash and can no longer continue playing.

When I first started playing the game against the computers, I would just be moving along the board collecting random chance cards and buying any property that I could. The opposing computers did the same thing. This caused the game to go on for many hours with no winner. I would usually get bored and leave the game. Eventually, my competitive nature kicked in, and I started developing strategies to win the game.

First, I knew the game was played with two dice, so the maximum number a computer could get on a dice roll was 12. The initial side of the board had six cheap properties. The first two properties were avoided like the plague by the other computers, and I was easily able to buy the properties at an auction for less than the original price. Once I secured the two properties in the geographic areas, I spent a small sum to build hotels in the area and collected large sums of rent money if the computer landed on my property. Then I bought the next block of middle properties that were on the same side of the board. To acquire these properties, I usually had to make savvy trades with the computer. Oftentimes, I had to overpay for the property, but the properties were needed in my overall strategy, and the rent collected would far outweigh the initial outlay of cash. I would then let the computer move along the rest of the board while they spend their money buying random properties. When the computers made it back to the initial side of the board, they either got lucky and landed on a chance card or a vacant spot. However, if they landed on any of my five hotels in the first twelve squares of the board, the computer had to pay rent and was close to losing since they spent so much money on the other sides of the board. As the computers were losing money, they could not afford the expensive properties anymore and were forced to auction off the property. I had so much money from the repeated rents I received that I was easily able to acquire the expensive properties at less than asking price. I finished building hotels in the expensive side of the board. Now if the computer lands on one of my expensive hotels, they will be instantly forced to withdraw from the game or sell all of their properties to remain in the game for a few more dice rolls.

With this new strategy, I kept winning in Monopoly World Edition. I thought maybe this strategy that helped me win in a real estate investing game can be applied to stock investing. Here are four similarities that I found:

1. Start by finding assets, in this case stocks, that are avoided by many and deemed worthless. These stocks are trading at throwaway prices, and it is easy to accumulate many shares.
2. Buy other assets that fit into your overall strategy that pay you rent. Some stocks pay cash dividends (rent) that can be reinvested to buy more of the same stock or the cash deposited to your account.
3. As you go through your investing journey, you do not need to buy every stock in the market.
4. Wait for moments when other investors panic and need cash immediately, so they sell wonderful assets at prices lower than the real value. Be ready to capitalize on this mistake (usually when the market gets irrational) and start taking large positions in wonderful companies.

Now, hopefully you too will be well positioned to "win" in this investing game. Just like in Monopoly, we need to break down the stock market into small easy to understand pieces. We have to first look at why a stock price moves and then understand the dynamics of the market.

What Drives Prices?

Have you ever looked at your portfolio and saw that the portfolio value changes every minute when the market is open? Have you ever watched CNBC or any financial news network and noticed the continuous run of ticker symbols with prices that change every second? You might be filled with joy to see the ticker of a stock you own to be up at the open and then you are saddened to see that ticker price is down the next second.

Let's take Starbucks (SBUX) as an example. On the bottom of the screen, CNBC shows changing ticker prices for Starbucks (SBUX) every second. Do you think all financial outlets have analysts at every Starbucks around the world dedicated to count how many cups of coffee are sold every second and report back? No, that would be ridiculous. Yet somehow the financial media can show changing prices of a stock in real time. So what do the intraday or day-to-day changes in a stock price mean?

The ticker price is really just buy and sell orders on the exchange every second. The buying and selling of a stock is based off people's emotional reactions to certain news events, macro factors, or fear and greed in certain situations. Real-time and short-term price fluctuations are based on sentiment, but over longer periods, stock prices are determined by earnings, cash flows, and book value.

Now you must be wondering why does the market go up or down for an extended period of time? Earnings, cash flows, and book value must be either increasing or decreasing, right? No two people can have the same feelings toward the market for an extended period of time. There may be events that can last months or years that overshadow the market. This news can cause people to respond in a certain manner that cause market movements in a certain direction for a long time. To get a better understanding of the market movements, we need to understand some key players in the market.

Dynamics of the Market

If you watch any financial program long enough, inevitably you will hear terms like "smart money" describe institutional or other investors with large amounts of money. Does being classified as an institution or having a large amount of money mean you are smart or always acting rationally in the stock market?

Think about a school of fish: if you throw a rock at a school of fish, all of the fish disperse. If you think about this, only a few fish that are in the vicinity of where the rock lands are in danger, but all of the fish in the school disperse as they are looking at the tails of the fish in front. The fish are not thinking if they are actually in danger; they are just following the crowd and moving frantically. Similarly, mutual fund managers and all institutional fund managers have to react the same way their peers do or risk subpar returns. A few subpar quarters will get the manager fired. Even if the manager thinks the stock is oversold and will rebound after the downturn, he or she will do what other managers do as it is safer to copy every other manager and get average returns. Going out on a limb and potentially being wrong is far too risky. Since large amounts of money are being taken out of the market or a certain sector, the market tends to move down. The smaller retail investors tend to see this movement and think the institutions know something and follow these moves.

Since investors like you and me are probably not managing money for clients, we do not have to buy or sell because everyone else is. In a letter to shareholders, Jeremy Grantham explains how one must resist the crowd and use fundamentals to make well-informed decisions. "The best way to resist is to do your own simple measurements of value, or find a reliable source (and check their calculations from time to time). Then hero-worship the numbers and try to ignore everything else. Ignore especially short-term news: the ebb and flow of economic and political news is irrelevant. Stock values are based on their entire future value of dividends and earnings going out many decades into the future. Shorter-term economic dips have no appreciable long-term effect on individual companies, let alone the broad asset classes that you should concentrate on. Leave those complexities to the professionals, who will on average lose money trying to decipher them" (Grantham 2012).

If you have selected a good company's stock, the management team will adjust and be able to rebound after the initial shock of the economic or political news. When these sudden shocks occur, it is important to ask yourself three things: First, what are the macro factors influencing the stock price? Second, will the bad news actually affect the company's earnings or long-term growth? Third, who is making a psychological misstep—you or other investors?

Now that you understand the reasons why the market is irrational, take advantage of these short-term movements and make your buy and sell decisions based on value, not what the crowd does. Unfortunately, the daily or monthly movements of the stock market is unpredictable, and there will be extreme highs or lows from time to time. Let's see what can cause these movements in the stock market and how to prepare ourselves for these shocks.

The Highs and Lows of the Market

In previous sections, we found that the market is inefficient. From time to time, the market will see extreme highs or lows. When the market reaches new highs, it is easy for me to avoid the hype and continue along with my investing journey. However, I still struggle with how should I act in a sell-off. Unlike housing markets, there are real-time updates of stock tickers, and it is excruciating to see my stock's price decline by the second. When the market is in a downturn, there is a constant barrage of glum forecasts in the media. It is human nature to make the bad news worse than it actually is. It is very easy to say I am a contrarian and when the market sells off, just start buying. After a few down days, my emotions will kick in, and I want to sell everything like most other people in the market.

One analogy that I came up with that has helped me during a sell-off is to think of the stock market like an actual supermarket. If a good product that you use every day is on sale, then you should buy more of the product. If the price rises, there is no need to buy the product as there is always another cheaper substitute product to buy instead. You do not need to buy a similar product if it is not a necessity. Just simply wait until your favorite product is back at a reasonable price. Similarly, the overall market will slump from time to time and drag your portfolio down too, but it's important not to get caught up in the fears and sell everything. Instead, one should look to buy more of the stock in the wonderful company that is on sale. The good news is that the occasional market drop is of little consequence to long-term investors. Attempting to sidestep the eventual downturn seems like a great idea, but it is extremely difficult to time the market successfully for years. Peter Lynch has stated, "Far more money has been lost by investors trying to anticipate corrections than has been lost in all the corrections combined" (Lynch and Rothchild 1995, p.112).

All of this is great in theory, but it is very hard to stay the course during a downturn. If you see a paper loss of 50% in your portfolio, it is easy to be tempted into selling to prevent further losses. There are some important lessons we can learn from history as stated by Peter Lynch: "One of the worst mistakes you can make is to switch into and out of stocks or stock mutual funds, hoping to avoid the upcoming correction. It's also a mistake to sit on your cash and wait for the upcoming correction before you invest in stocks. In trying to time the market to sidestep the bears, people often miss out on the chance to run with the bulls. A review of the S&P 500 going back to 1954 shows how expensive it is to be out of stocks during the short stretches when they make their biggest jumps. If you kept all your money in stocks throughout these four decades, your annual return on investment was 11.5 percent. Yet if you were out of stocks for the forty most profitable months during these forty years, your return on investment dropped to 2.7 percent" (Lynch and Rothchild 1995, p.112).

Wow! Putting my money on the sidelines and trying to sidestep the market can actually cost me in the long run. If I am able to withstand temporary pain and remain disciplined in my investing approach, the long-term gain will outweigh the short-term pain.

I do want to point out the market is not always destined to slump. Sometimes there are periods when the market is overly euphoric, but that usually ends in disaster. For example, back in the 2000s, any stock with a dot-com, house prices in 2007, GameStop and the meme stocks in 2021, and most of the penny cryptos in 2021–2022 went up 100+%, only to collapse. Many people poured all their money in these assets, thinking they would be overnight millionaires. However, most people had no idea what or why they were buying the asset other than it is going up. It's easy to be tempted to join the mass frenzy, but if you cannot understand what you are buying, it is safer not to buy. Many people told me to buy a certain asset as it was marching up to over 100%. I asked two simple questions why is this asset better than any other asset? Second, is there any real earnings or anything of value that I can use to value the company or asset? I was usually met with "I don't know, but who cares, it is going up." The media did the same thing to hype up all these asset bubbles. Since I could not figure out what was going on, I did not invest. Ultimately like all bubbles, the bubble popped, and investors were left holding the bag once the hype went away. In any up or down movement, it is important to understand that the market is controlled by investor psychology in the short-term.

Psychology

No matter what stage you are at in your investing journey, more likely than not someone has given you the timeless Warren Buffett advice, "we simply attempt to be fearful when others are greedy and to be greedy only when others are fearful" (Buffett 1986). Well how does one know when to be greedy or a fearful investor? We first need to be able to spot the changes in the greed/fear attitudes among other investors, and then we can respond in the proper way.

I have seen many folks in the media during 2021 clamoring for the Fed to raise rates because inflation was getting out of control. Then in 2022, when the Fed said they plan on raising rates, the same people in the media started saying the Fed will raise rates too fast and will blow out the economy. I thought to myself, why aren't these figures in the media happy that the Fed is going to raise rates as they suggested a few months back? If someone agrees with your point of view, would you say the person is not agreeing with me in the right way? Why is there more doomsday scenarios than actual realistic situations in the media? The only answer I can come up with is that…fear sells.

In his book *The Psychology of Money*, author Morgan Housel made some interesting observations regarding how we react to news.

> Say we'll have a big recession and newspapers will call you. Say we're headed for average growth and no one particularly cares. Say we're nearing the

next Great Depression and you'll get on TV. But mention that good times are ahead, or markets have room to run, or that a company has huge potential, and a common reaction from commentators and spectators alike is that you are either a salesman or comically aloof of risks.

The investing newsletter industry has known this for years, and is now populated by prophets of doom despite operating in an environment where the stock market has gone up 17,000-fold in the last century (including dividends).

Stocks rising 1% might be briefly mentioned in the evening news. But a 1% fall will be reported in bold, all-caps letters usually written in blood red. The asymmetry is hard to avoid.

And while few question or try to explain why the market went up—isn't it supposed to go up?—there is almost always an attempt to explain why it went down. (Housel 2020, p. 187)

Let's say there are two articles about a stock you own. The first has the headline XYZ stock will go up one hundred times in the next five years on strong demand. It is natural to say I know and that's why I bought the stock. Then you brush the article aside and move on. On the other hand, the second article reads "Accounting Fraud: XYZ stock to decline by 50%." You want to know more and decide to read this article on the dangers of XYZ stock.

Risky Views

It is hard not to have an emotional reaction to certain market moving developments that are constantly brought up in the media. In his book *Mastering the Market Cycle: Getting the Odds on Your Side*, Howard Marks shares an important story with readers. "A few years ago my friend Jon Brooks supplied this great illustration of skewed interpretation at work. Here's how investors react to events when they're feeling good about life (which usually means the market has been rising): Strong data: economy strengthening—stocks rally Weak data: Fed likely to ease—stocks rally Data as expected: low volatility—stocks rally Banks make $4 billion: business conditions favorable—stocks rally Banks lose $4 billion: bad news out of the way—stocks rally Oil spikes: growing global economy contributing to demand—stocks rally Oil drops: more purchasing power for the consumer—stocks rally Dollar plunges: great for exporters—stocks rally Dollar strengthens: great for companies that buy from abroad—stocks rally Inflation spikes: will cause assets to appreciate—stocks rally Inflation drops: improves quality of earnings—stocks rally Of course, the same behavior also applies in the opposite direction. When psychology is negative and markets have been falling for a while, everything is capable of being interpreted negatively. Strong economic data is seen as likely to make the Fed withdraw stimulus by raising interest rates, and weak data is taken to mean companies will have trouble meeting earnings forecasts. In other words, it's not the data or events; it's the interpretation. And that fluctuates with swings in psychology" (Marks 2018).

The main thing you will notice in changing psychology is a change in attitude toward risk. When there are long periods of good times, many investors start becoming risk-averse, optimistic, greedy, and pay premium prices for risky returns. Investors think these good times will go on forever and start saying that this time is different because geopolitical, new developments in technology, or changes in the economy have changed the old rules of investing. The herd of investors will say don't wait too long or you might miss the opportunity as this stock can only go higher. On the other hand, when things are bad for a long period of time, the sentiment shifts to investors being very cautious, frantically selling, or leaving investing in general. The statements are now more in line with stocks will just keep going lower, so get out before it goes to zero.

Nothing goes on forever, and you must avoid succumbing to this peer pressure. In Howard Marks's 2008 memo to shareholders on "The Limits to Negativism," Marks states, "Following the beliefs of the herd—and swinging with the pendulum—will give you average performance in the long run and can get you killed at the extremes" (Marks 2008, p. 2). By blindly following every other investor that participates in the market, you cannot outperform the market. If all investors are acting in one way, that is the new average. The cohort of momentum investors tend to apply optimism at the top and pessimism at the bottom. This more often than not is the time when stock prices have diverged from intrinsic value and create a buying or selling opportunity. This extreme form of herd mentality that takes over the market almost always leads to the greatest mistakes in investing. Therefore, it is crucial to develop a contrarian mindset approach.

Contrarian Mindset

When investors in the market are overjoyed, are highly reckless, and overconfident, we should be cautious. People tend to exaggerate upside potential and believe old evaluations do not matter anymore. When other investors feel that there is no risk and are constantly buying stocks sending valuations into the stratosphere, this is actually the most risky time to buy stocks. Since your holdings have all risen way above fair value, you should look to sell or trim positions that you no longer want to hold. On the other hand, when others are frightened into panic selling and say it is risky to buy stocks, this is indeed the best time to add to or start new positions. Since the market has dropped the prices of wonderful companies so low, their stocks are trading well below the margin of safety price. There is no risk in being aggressive and to start buying stocks. Remember, nothing goes on forever, and prices eventually reverse to the median.

A key to the success of Berkshire Hathaway can be found in this quote by Warren Buffett, "The less the prudence with which others conduct their affairs, the greater the prudence with which we must conduct our own" (Buffet 2018, February 24). This quote highlights Buffett's thought process and how he is able to think rationally when the market sentiment is at either extreme. When the market is irrational, one must take advantage of the potential opportunities that are present. There are two examples when the market became very irrational and wonderful stocks were selling at deep discounts. Buffett immediately seized the opportunities. Marry Buffet states, "He could never have made his 2000 purchase of 8% of H&R Block for approximately $28 a share or the much discussed 1974 purchase of 1.7 million shares of the Washington Post Company for approximately $6.14 a share. H&R Block now trades at approximately $60 a share and the Post now trades at approximately $500 a share. His pretax rate of return on his H&R Block purchase, after one year, was approximately 41% and his total pretax return on the Post purchase, after twenty-seven years, is approximately 8,468% which equates to a pretax annual compounding rate of return of approximately 17.8%" (Buffett and Clark 2002, p. 11).

Don't fall into the habit of saying just because a herd of investors is doing something, it is automatically wrong. Allow value to dictate your actions in the stock market not the volatile price movements in the market caused by changing attitudes of the herd. When there is uncertainty in the market that can lead to turbulence in the market, that is when you should start making a list of companies that you want to own and meet the criteria of great companies. All you have to do is wait until the price of the stock on your shopping list falls within your margin of safety price. If the uncertainty leads to prices surging, reevaluate your holdings and decide if you want to sell any stock that is trading drastically above intrinsic value.

Always Stay in the Market

People may think it's dangerous to be invested in stocks during crashes and corrections, but it's nearly impossible to predict when these crashes or corrections will occur. Crashes or corrections usually occur due to various unknown geopolitical, economic, or other unknown events. These events usually cause uncertainty in the market and send shockwaves of fear among investors. Most people start to panic and tend to sell their stocks during the turbulent times only to see the same stock rebound later. The investor regrets that they sold too early and wishes they held their stocks through thick and thin.

> While reading Peter Lynch's book *Learn to Earn*, I came across a powerful example of why one should be invested at all times. Let's look back to a booming 5-year period during the 1980s. Over that span, the market gained 26.3% a year. However, the market did not go up in a straight line, and there were corrections along the way. It was found that most of the annual gains occurred on 40 days of the 1,276 days the stock market was open. If an investor held throughout those 5 years, he or she would have doubled their money and more. However, if the investor sold during every correction and was out of the market during those 40 days, the annual return fell to a meager 4.3%. At that time, a CD in the bank was returning more than 4.3% and was less riskier than equity investments. If you are young, the best course of action is to only invest money that you do not need to cover your daily expenses and always remain fully invested in the market. No one can accurately predict the exact day the market will crash or when the start of a bull market will occur. To get the full benefit of those magical and unpredictable stretches when stocks make most of their gains, one has to be able to withstand the unpredictable loss and have the fortitude to hold on for the inevitable rebound (Lynch and Rothchild 1995, p. 65).

During the 2018 Berkshire Hathaway meeting, Warren Buffett had everyone in the audience imagine they were embarking on an investing journey on March 11th of 1942. Despite the negative backdrop, you believed in America and decided to put $10,000 in the S&P 500. You treat the investment similar to buying a farm that you hold for your life. Your initial $10,000 investment is worth $51 million today.

If you had invested $1 million with a tax-free pension fund or college endowment, your investment would have grown to about $5.3 billion. However, most funds charge a fee of about 1%. Over the seventy-seven years, if the funds matched the annual 11.8% return of the S&P 500 but after fees returned 10.8%, the projected $5.3 billion is now half as much at $2.65 billion.

Now if you were spooked out of stocks due to a doomsday scenario, and instead used the $10,000 to buy gold. You would have three hundred ounces of gold that would have appreciated to about $400,000. For every dollar you had made in an American business, you'd have less than a penny of gain by having a store of value like gold. Still, people tell you to run to gold or other inflation hedges every time you get scared by the turbulence in the market.

From 1942 to 2018, Americans have seen fourteen US presidents, a world war, 9/11, and the Cuban Missile Crisis, to name a few geopolitical events. Each event caused turbulence in the market; however, all one had to do was believe that America will progress as it has ever since 1776.

The main takeaway is that even if you do not have $10,000 to invest, by putting a small sum into a market index fund, you can still see extraordinary results. In 1942, Buffett had $114.75 that he used to buy his first stock; if he had bought the S&P 500 instead with reinvested dividends, his stake would have grown to $606,811 by January 31, 2019 (Berkshire Hathaway Annual Meeting 2018).

It may be harder to remain fully invested as one approaches retirement age, and a person may want to withdraw all of their money during a bear market. Instead of completely selling out of the market, there should be more emphasis on risk management and moving to safer assets.

SO YOU WANT TO BE A SUPERINVESTOR?

Tune Out the Noise

Some of the information that I hear in the media is very important information providing different views so I can approach investment problems from all angles. However, a lot of the information is just noise and speculation to illicit an emotional reaction. This information overload can drive anyone crazy. How should I keep my focus? What is the best way to tune out the noise? Media pundits focus on too many macro variables (general view on stocks, rates, FX, commodities, GDP), these variables are just talking about the overall economy. They have no impact on individual stocks and should not influence your investing decisions.

Even a pupil of Warren Buffet, Guy Spier, moved away from New York with the constant forecasts from analysts to Zurich so he could get away from the noise and the pressure cooker environment. Spier said he could think and invest rationally in Zurich since he was not bombarded by forecasts. I am not saying that you must move away from New York and live in Omaha or Zurich, but you need to find what works for you so you do not get caught up in the noise and make irrational investment decisions. When the market is suffering more than a 200-point drop at the open, I don't even watch the news as it will just be filled with analysts stating doomsday forecasts. On the other hand, if the market is up more than 200 points at the open, I limit myself to only listen to analysts that I think act rationally and are not overly exuberant. The most important things are to avoid the noise, buy right and hold for the long-term, and seize on the opportunity provided by market gyrations.

Sometimes it is impossible to avoid the media no matter how hard you try. There are a few people in the media I respect. What I look for is an analyst that is rational and constructs their portfolio similar to mine. These analysts make generalizations on the market or an industry and tend to be buyers rather than sellers during a dip. Other analysts come on TV and have a boastful tone, give doom and gloom or carefree forecasts, so I choose not to listen to them. It is really important to see what an analyst does in a situation rather than what they say. I do not believe any analyst on TV has a malicious intent. The advice or forecasts that they give is tailored to having a short-term investing approach. Before listening to an analyst and hastily acting on advice, take a step back and think about your financial goals. Ask yourself, how will this advice help or hurt me in my financial journey based on my time horizon?

CHAPTER 4
You Need to Start Now!

Warren Buffett once said, "If you don't find a way to make money while you sleep, you will work until you die." In the distant future, I want to be able to retire and live a financially free life. I do not want to run out of money in my elder years and be forced back into work when I am eighty. Buffett gives us a dire warning, if we do not figure out how to secure our financial future now, we may suffer dire consequences later.

Can I Have a Good Retirement or Future Plans?

If you are young and just starting your career, retirement seems too far in the future. If you are in the middle of your career and starting to think about retirement, will you be able to enjoy your money in the future? Maybe you are near or already retired and are planning on leaving money for future generations, will you be able to leave a substantial sum? Maybe you are in school and do not have money to invest right now, well you can learn the skills and be ready to invest once you have money in the future. If you are in your forties or fifties, then you should definitely read this before it is too late. There may be some upcoming life events you want to save for. No matter what age you are or if you are a novice or experienced investor looking to do better, the tips and lessons learned from the rest of this book will help you. Hopefully both you and I can join the ranks of the Superinvestors. Whatever your financial goals are for the future, the most important thing you can do is to start to invest and let your money compound over time.

Most investment advisors will do everything in their power to scare you into thinking you cannot plan for your financial future on your own. They claim to be your friend and have your best interest in mind. Let's take a step back. If you have ever watched the closing or opening bell of the stock market, there are always brokers, traders, advisors, and other members of the investment community cheering. The Dow Jones Industrial average (a popular stock index) may be down 1,000 points, yet these "friends" are still cheering. Why? The advisors' clients just lost a ton of money. There goes your yacht! Most advisors do not care, because they are still getting paid a flat fee based on the amount of money managed, not their performance. The advisor is getting a yacht that you paid for no matter what the market does.

Can I Do This on My Own?

You may be thinking to yourself now, I need to start investing, but I can't do this on my own. All of the financial advisors or professional money managers are far better at making money than I am, so why not just let them manage my money? Of course, the financial services industry that makes $100 billion a year from fees has convinced you to think that you cannot manage your own money, and they should be in charge of your future for a price.

Some money managers are good and actually beat the market by a hefty margin, but most money managers will underperform, match, or slightly beat the market. If the money manager beats the market by a very small margin, you are actually underperforming the market as you need to account for the 1–2% fees the money manager takes from you. This is not to say that these money managers are acting with a malicious intent; it is just the way the industry is set up.

Two great Warren Buffett quotes you should keep in mind if you are on the fence about selecting a money manager: "When trillions of dollars are managed by Wall Streeters charging high fees, it will usually be the managers who reap outsized profits, not the clients" (Melloy 2017). Second, "If returns are going to be 7 or 8 percent and you're paying 1 percent for fees, that makes an enormous difference in how much money you're going to have in retirement" (Martin 2018). Now if the money manager can provide value and has very good insights, then you must evaluate based on your financial needs if selecting a money manager is best for you.

You may be too busy to do the research on individual companies and, in that case, just put your money in a low-cost index fund. The index fund will give you market returns and is passively managed (the fund manager is not actively trading daily), so the fund does not have the high management fees. If you happen to be lucky and find a money manager that takes advantage of the inefficiencies of the market, then by all means, invest with them as they are providing value. More likely you will have the manager who believes in theories like efficient market theory or the only way to avoid risk is diversification. If the money manager says something like this, run!

My goal in this book is to demystify the stock market so you can manage your own money and will not need a money manager to decide if you can live comfortably in retirement. In the following chapters, I will show you the secret to investing, how to go about selecting stocks, lessons we can learn from history, and when to think about selling stocks. We can all understand and conquer the market!

PART 3

Understanding the Compounding Machine

CHAPTER 5
You Just Need to Compound Money!

In 2020, I started reading a lot about the new way of value investing that Berkshire Hathaway uses called focus investing. Across the various books discussing the topic, they all mentioned compound interest. What was compound interest, and how can that help my investments? Compounding occurs when an asset has capital gains, dividends, or interest reinvested to generate more earnings in the future. I found a compound interest calculator on bankrate.com. You input your starting amount, years to save, rate of return, additional contributions made over a certain timeframe, and compounding frequency. Then you can see a detailed report of how your investment will grow over time. The report will provide a breakdown of the interest and your contributions that make up your total balance for every year. I kept playing with the inputs and saw how the final results could be life-changing.

The stock market is a very complex and fickle beast. You have the opportunity to obtain the mighty sword, compound interest, to slay the beast. Albert Einstein called compound interest the eighth wonder of the world. Have you ever wondered how Warren Buffett became the best investor of all time? Compound interest played a big factor. Edgar Wachenheim, a value-oriented hedge fund manager, pointed out, "Compounding is one of my favorite words. Compounding is powerful. Warren Buffett did not become one of the wealthiest men in the world by suddenly striking gold in a single highly successful investment, but rather by compounding the value of Berkshire Hathaway at a 20 percent or so rate for 45 years. If an investor can achieve an average annual return of 20 percent, then, after 45 years, an initial investment of $1 million will appreciate to $3.6 billion. Wow!" (Compoundingquotes). This compounding mechanism can be used by anyone even if you do not have a million dollars. Let's look how this life-changing phenomenon can affect your investments.

In the first part of the table, you can see the person started with a $10,000 portfolio and held the positions through thick and thin. The investor never sold any of the positions and did not generate a short-term tax hit. The person compounded money at an annual rate of 15%. This is a hypothetical example, so I chose a 15% return for every year. In the real world, your returns will fluctuate year over year, but it is important to take the average rate of return in your compounding calculations. When the person retired and sold in year 29, the investor incurred a 15% long-term capital gains tax. The initial $10,000 has grown to $500,656.12, and you can receive $425557.70 after tax.

Now let's say the person was finicky and held positions from January 2 to December 31 and then churned the portfolio to get the hottest stocks for the next year. As you see in the second part of the table, the person obtained the same 15% return, but all the buying and selling created a short-term capital gains tax of 20% every year. By only reinvesting the after-tax amount and not compounding the initial $10,000, the final value only becomes $238,838.66. That's a $186,719.04 difference in potential return if the person moves in and out of stocks.

Warren Buffett has given great advice on how to maximize the power of compounding: "The nature of compound interest is it behaves like a snowball of sticky snow. And the trick is to have a very long hill, which means either starting very young or living very—to be very old." His partner Charlie Munger adds, "The first rule of compounding: Never interrupt it unnecessarily" (Compoundingquotes). For compounding to work, you need time in investments and to avoid making buy or sell decisions based on emotions.

This is not to say that there is no downside to compounding. If you have made a mistake in selecting a stock, and the investment returns 0% or negative returns it is best to sell and try again because compounding a 0 is still 0.

The most important thing to understand is that compounding money takes time and every move you make derails the maximum result. This is a true test of patience. Professor Christopher Begg who teaches Security Analysis from Ben Graham and David Dodd at Columbia University, is amazed why this simple fact is neglected. "Investing is simply maximizing the rate of compounding for as long as capital can be employed net of fees and taxes. What strikes us as strange is how little we hear about compounding with regard to investing. We find the short-term perspective affecting the collective market psyche is focused on direction and immediate results that often limit the ability to truly accomplish outstanding rates of compounding" (Compoundingquotes). Now that you know how compounding can work wonders, how should we go about what to put in our compounding machines?

ASHRAY JHA

	A	B	C	D	E	F
	Starting investment:$10000	15% return			Starting investment:$10000	15% retu
	year 1	$ 11,500.00			Year 1	$ 11,500
	year 2	$ 13,225.00			Year 2	$ 12,88
	year 3	$ 15,208.75			Year 3	$ 14,42
	year 4	$ 17,490.06			Year 4	$ 16,15
	year 5	$ 20,113.57			Year 5	$ 18,09
	year 6	$ 23,130.61			Year 6	$ 20,26
	year 7	$ 26,600.20			Year 7	$ 22,69
	year 8	$ 30,590.23			Year 8	$ 25,42
	year 9	$ 35,178.76			Year 9	$ 28,47
	year 10	$ 40,455.58			Year 10	$ 31,89
	year 11	$ 46,523.91			Year 11	$ 35,71
	year 12	$ 53,502.50			Year 12	$ 40,00
	year 13	$ 61,527.88			Year 13	$ 44,80
	year 14	$ 70,757.06			Year 14	$ 50,18
	year 15	$ 81,370.62			Year 15	$ 56,20
	year 16	$ 93,576.21			Year 16	$ 62,94
	year 17	$ 107,612.64			Year 17	$ 70,49
	year 18	$ 123,754.54			Year 18	$ 78,95
	year 19	$ 142,317.72			Year 19	$ 88,43
	year 20	$ 163,665.37			Year 20	$ 99,04
	year 21	$ 188,215.18			Year 21	$ 110,93
	year 22	$ 216,447.46			Year 22	$ 124,24
	year 23	$ 248,914.58			Year 23	$ 139,15
	year 24	$ 286,251.76			Year 24	$ 155,85
	year 25	$ 329,189.53			Year 25	$ 174,55
	year 26	$ 378,567.96			Year 26	$ 195,50
	year 27	$ 435,353.15			Year 27	$ 218,96
	year 28	$ 500,656.12			Year 28	$ 245,23
	sell at 15% tax	$ 425,557.70			sell	

SO YOU WANT TO BE A SUPERINVESTOR?

G	H	I	J	K
nd 20% tax on gain	remaining investment			
300.00	$ 11,200.00			
336.00	$ 12,544.00			
376.32	$ 14,049.28			
421.48	$ 15,735.19			
472.06	$ 17,623.42			
528.70	$ 19,738.23			
592.15	$ 22,106.81			
663.20	$ 24,759.63			
742.79	$ 27,730.79			
831.92	$ 31,058.48			
931.75	$ 34,785.50			
1,043.56	$ 38,959.76			
1,168.79	$ 43,634.93			
1,309.05	$ 48,871.12			
1,466.13	$ 54,735.66			
1,642.07	$ 61,303.94			
1,839.12	$ 68,660.41			
2,059.81	$ 76,899.66			
2,306.99	$ 86,127.62			
2,583.83	$ 96,462.93			
2,893.89	$ 108,038.48			
3,241.15	$ 121,003.10			
3,630.09	$ 135,523.47			
4,065.70	$ 151,786.29			
4,553.59	$ 170,000.64			
5,100.02	$ 190,400.72			
5,712.02	$ 213,248.81			
6,397.46	$ 238,838.66		difference	$ 186,719.04

CHAPTER 6
You Can Choose the Best Asset Class!

Throughout your investing journey, you will definitely encounter people who try to sway you into investing in a particular asset class. Every so often the stock market slumps, and people start saying get out of stocks and invest in safety plays like bonds. When inflation spikes, people start saying things like increase your allocation in gold to hedge against inflation. When the stock market is acting normally, there is always a debate that investments in real estate are a better choice than stock investments. Just like stocks, all investment assets go through boom and bust cycles, and in any short period of time, one asset class may look better than another. This made me wonder, do I really want to churn my portfolio every year to hold the best performing asset class of the past year? There is no guarantee the best performing asset class from the previous year will repeat or have more success in the following year. I know the cliché many financial advisors say is to diversify your holdings into various asset classes in order to eliminate risk in your portfolio. That means I should hold a few items of each asset class in my portfolio. If I hold five different assets for the long-term, I can assume only one out of five will be successful, and the other four assets will provide average returns in any given year. In previous chapters, we have found that excessive diversification does not really reduce market risk but can diminish investment returns. Instead of holding five different asset classes, and capping my maximum return for any given year, I should start my search by determining which asset class is the best to hold over a long period of time.

Differing from financial advisors, Warren Buffett has said, "Diversification is protection against ignorance. It makes little sense if you know what you are doing," and "Diversification may preserve wealth, but concentration builds wealth." I am just starting my real investing journey, so I do need a concentrated portfolio to build wealth, and I should not be ignorant and diversify. But how do I know which asset class to hold in a concentrated portfolio?

Every so often, I will be watching the financial news, and when one asset class is not doing well, members of the media will say get out of the falling class and jump into another rising asset class. These frequent moves in and out of the market seems like a good idea, but it is interrupting compounding unnecessarily. Hey, that's what Charlie Munger told us not to do. There is merit to all kinds of investment assets, and at the end of the day, you have to make a decision based on your risk tolerance and your financial goals. In the next few sections, I will compare each asset class to stocks and try to determine which asset class is better to hold over the long-term. In any asset class, one specific investment can outperform another, so I will be utilizing market averages for each asset class as applicable.

Professor Aswath Damodaran from NYU composed a table of the annual returns of stocks, short- and long-term government securities, real estate, and corporate bonds from 1928 to 2021. FRED the Federal Reserve website provided the yields for long-term treasury bonds, short-term treasury bills, and medium risk Baa corporate bonds. For treasury bonds, the yield was converted to a total return by repricing the bond at par with the prior year's yield. This same approach was used to calculate the total return for corporate bonds. T-bills are short-term securities and should not see any changes to their price, so the average rate returned for the year was used.

Robert Schiller had collected the housing data from 1928 in his website, which is now widely known as the Case-Shiller Index. Please note that the S&P 500 was created in 1957, so the data from 1928–1956 was backdated using other indices of large market cap companies that existed prior to 1957. Since the S&P 500 provided dividends, the total return was calculated by adding the change in price of the index and the dividends to find the annual return.

Unfortunately, there is a subtle inflation tax or a rise in prices of goods. This rise in the price of goods can erode the value of your investment dollars. The FRED website reports the Consumer Price Index for the rise in prices of goods. To get the real or inflation adjusted returns, we remove the inflation rate from the nominal return of the asset (1+ Nominal Rate)/ (1+Inflation Rate) -1.

At the end of the day, an investment is sold for cash to purchase other items. The items that you want to purchase are subject to inflation, and the price of the good rises over time. When you sell your investment, you will have the total return amount after taxes, but that same amount of money will not be worth as much in the future. Therefore, I calculated the effects of inflation on each asset class to determine the decrease in purchasing power over time.

Another popular investment class is the stated inflation hedge gold. Using Macrotrends website, I was able to get the annual returns for gold from 1969 to 2021. I calculated the real returns to see the impact of inflation on gold.

To make it easier to see the change in dollar value, I took a hypothetical $500 investment and calculated the hypothetical and real value of your investment for each year. Now let's take a look how each asset class performs over time.

Real Estate versus Stocks

There are many people who are very successful in real estate investing, and I can see the allure of trying to be a real estate mogul. If you go on YouTube, there are hundreds of people telling you to join their real estate investing course, and they will show you how to be successful too. All you need to do is buy their $99.99 training course to maybe learn something new. These sales people are so convincing that even I thought that real estate investing was a sure thing. I must buy now or miss out on this golden opportunity! Luckily I took a step back and realized during the housing crisis of 2008, both stocks and real estate investments were affected negatively. If real estate investments can go down too, is real estate really a safe haven when there is a crisis in the economy? I came across a Barron's article and research from NYU professor Aswath Damodaran that proved real estate investing is not better than buying stocks.

> Stocks as measured by the S&P 500 index returned 12.47% annually from 1972 to 2021, versus 5.41% for residential housing based on the Case-Shiller Index, through last October, a span that encompasses inflation's liftoff after the dollar's link to gold was severed. Looking at 2012–2021, which takes in to account the recovery from the housing bust that precipitated the 2007–09 financial crisis, stocks returned an average 16.98%, versus 7.38% for housing. (Forsyth 2022)

The total return data for each year is located in a table in the appendix, but to make it easier to see, I created a chart in excel that shows the returns of the S&P 500 compared to real estate. I also added two trend lines to make the long-term trends apparent.

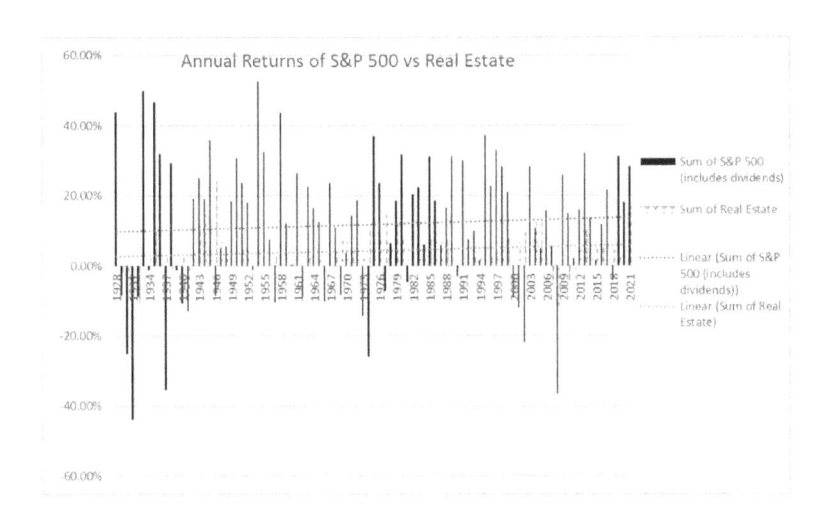

Annual Returns of S&P 500 vs Real Estate

S&P 500 1930–1939 avg	4.27%	Real Estate 1930–1939 avg	-1.05%
S&P 500 1940–1949 avg	9.64%	Real Estate 1940–1949 avg	8.56%
S&P 500 1950–1959 avg	20.93%	Real Estate 1950–1959 avg	3.09%
S&P 500 1960–1969 avg	8.60%	Real Estate 1960–1969 avg	2.18%
S&P 500 1970–1979 avg	7.52%	Real Estate 1970–1979 avg	8.80%
S&P 500 1980–1989 avg	17.95%	Real Estate 1980–1989 avg	5.90%
S&P 500 1990–1999 avg	18.82%	Real Estate 1990–1999 avg	2.70%
S&P 500 2000–2009 avg	1.16%	Real Estate 2000–2009 avg	4.30%
S&P 500 2009–2019 avg	14.02%	Real Estate 2009–2019 avg	3.86%
S&P 500 1928–2021 max	52.56%	Real Estate 1928–2021 max	24.10%
S&P 500 1928–2021 min	-43.84%	Real Estate 1928–2021 min	-12.00%
S&P 500 1928–2021 avg	11.82%	Real Estate 1928–2021 avg	4.36%
S&P 500 1928–2021 standard deviation	19.46%	Real Estate 1928–2021 standard deviation	6.26%

The solid black lines are the yearly returns from the S&P 500, and the diamond bars are for the yearly returns from real estate investments. There are trendlines for both asset classes, and the trendline for the S&P 500 is much higher than the trendline for real estate investments. The maximum return in the S&P 500 during the years between 1928–2021 was 52.56%, but the maximum return for real estate investments during the same time period was only 24.10%. The minimum return for the S&P 500 during the years between 1928–2021 was -43.84%, but the minimum return for real estate investments during the same time period was better at -12% The average return in the S&P 500 from 1928 to 2021 was 11.82%, opposed to real estate with an average return of 4.36%. As you can see from the table, every decade did not produce the average return. Every year varied and was either higher or lower than average. Thus, I calculated the standard deviation to see the average variance among asset classes. The standard deviation of the S&P 500 was 19.46%, opposed to real estate investments with a standard deviation of 6.26%. In seven of the nine decades from 1930–2019, the S&P 500 produced a higher average return than real estate investments. When the market was negative, real estate investments did better. However, more often than not the market index of the S&P 500 was positive and much higher than real estate returns. Also from the wide differences in the maximum, minimum, and standard deviation we see that investments in real estate are safer in the sense that they are more likely to provide average and steady returns opposed to the S&P 500 index. However, the S&P 500 had an average more than double real estate, but the returns varied significantly from average in either direction. Now let's take a look at how a hypothetical $500 would grow if invested in either asset class.

If you were to invest $500 in the S&P 500 or in real estate investments in 1928 and held until 2021, your returns would be as follows:

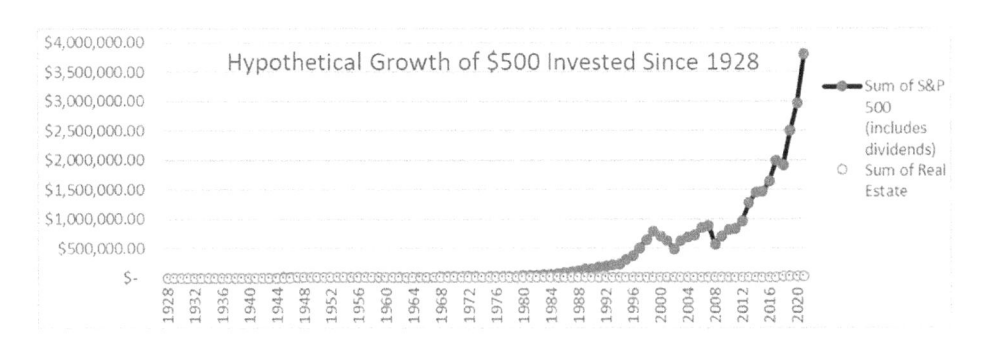

Hypothetical Growth of $500 Invested Since 1928

	1938	1948	1958	1968	1978	1988	1998	2008	2018	2021
S&P 500	$607.66	$1,148.96	$7,179.20	$18,471.15	25,408.84	$113,362.01	$647,961.26	$565,151.11	$1,914,354.69	$3,808,554.17
Real Estate	$445.98	$960.24	$1,295.14	$1,500.83	$3,254.50	$6,276.90	$7,918.07	$13,064.60	$17,539.66	$23,446.74

Starting from 1928, the initial $500 investment in the S&P 500 has ballooned to $3,808,554.17 at the end of 2021, but that same $500 investment in real estate only grew to $23,446.74 by the end of 2021. The difference in the final values is astronomical. Why is there so much difference between the two values? The difference is due to compounding over a long time. Compounding money at an average rate of 11.82% instead of 4.36% for ninety-three years makes a major difference!

Now we can't forget about our pesky little friend inflation that alters the annual returns of our investment.

Real Returns of S&P 500 vs Real Estate

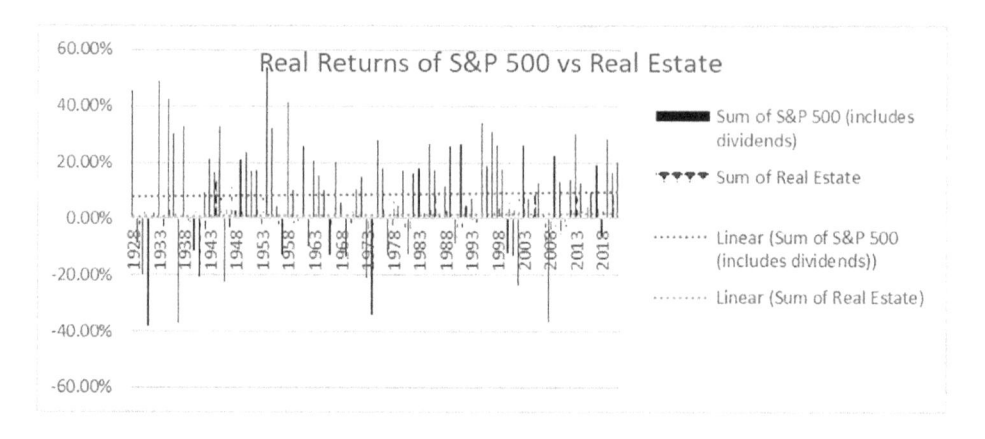

Inflation 1930–1939 avg	-1.92%
Inflation 1940–1949 avg	5.51%
Inflation 1950–1959 avg	2.24%
Inflation 1960–1969 avg	2.53%
Inflation 1970–1979 avg	7.41%
Inflation 1980–1989 avg	5.14%
Inflation 1990–1999 avg	2.94%
Inflation 2000–2009 avg	2.53%
Inflation 2009–2019 avg	1.76%
Inflation 1928–2021 max	18.13%
Inflation 1928–2021 min	-10.27%
Inflation 1928–2021 avg	3.08%
Inflation 1928–2021 standard deviation	3.96%

These are the average inflation rates for the decade. To get the real rate, I took (1+nominal rate)/(1+inflation rate)-1=real rate for each year. Then I took the average to get the real rate for the decade.

Note: The yearly data for rates of each asset class and inflation are listed in appendix tables.

S&P 500 1930–1939 avg	5.72%	Real Estate 1930–1939 avg	0.88%
S&P 500 1940–1949 avg	4.56%	Real Estate 1940–1949 avg	3.00%
S&P 500 1950–1959 avg	18.40%	Real Estate 1950–1959 avg	0.86%
S&P 500 1960–1969 avg	6.04%	Real Estate 1960–1969 avg	-0.34%
S&P 500 1970–1979 avg	0.40%	Real Estate 1970–1979 avg	1.32%
S&P 500 1980–1989 avg	12.27%	Real Estate 1980–1989 avg	0.81%
S&P 500 1990–1999 avg	15.53%	Real Estate 1990–1999 avg	-0.20%
S&P 500 2000–2009 avg	-1.43%	Real Estate 2000–2009 avg	1.70%
S&P 500 2009–2019 avg	12.06%	Real Estate 2009–2019 avg	2.08%
S&P 500 1928–2021 max	53.71%	Real Estate 1928–2021 max	13.96%
S&P 500 1928–2021 min	-38.07%	Real Estate 1928–2021 min	-16.66%
S&P 500 1928–2021 avg	8.60%	Real Estate 1928–2021 avg	1.27%
S&P 500 1928–2021 standard deviation	19.34%	Real Estate 1928–2021 standard deviation	5.03%

We still see the same long-term trend in the S&P 500 and real estate investments as the annual returns are impacted the same way for both asset classes after adjusting for inflation. The maximum return in the S&P 500 during the years between 1928–2021 was 53.71%, but the maximum return for real estate investments during the same time period was only 13.96%. The minimum return in the S&P 500 during the years between 1928–2021 was -38.07%, but the minimum return for real estate investments during the same time period was better at -16.66% The average return in the S&P 500 from 1928 to 2021 is 8.6%, opposed to real estate with an average return of 1.27%. As you can see from the table, every decade did not produce the average return. Every year varied and was either higher or lower than average. Thus, I calculated the standard deviation to see the average variance among asset classes. The standard deviation of the S&P 500 is 19.34%, opposed to real estate investments with a standard deviation of 5.03%. In seven of the nine decades from 1930–2019, the S&P 500 produced a higher average return than real estate investments. Once we begin compounding the inflation rate over time, there is a stark difference as the purchasing power decreases.

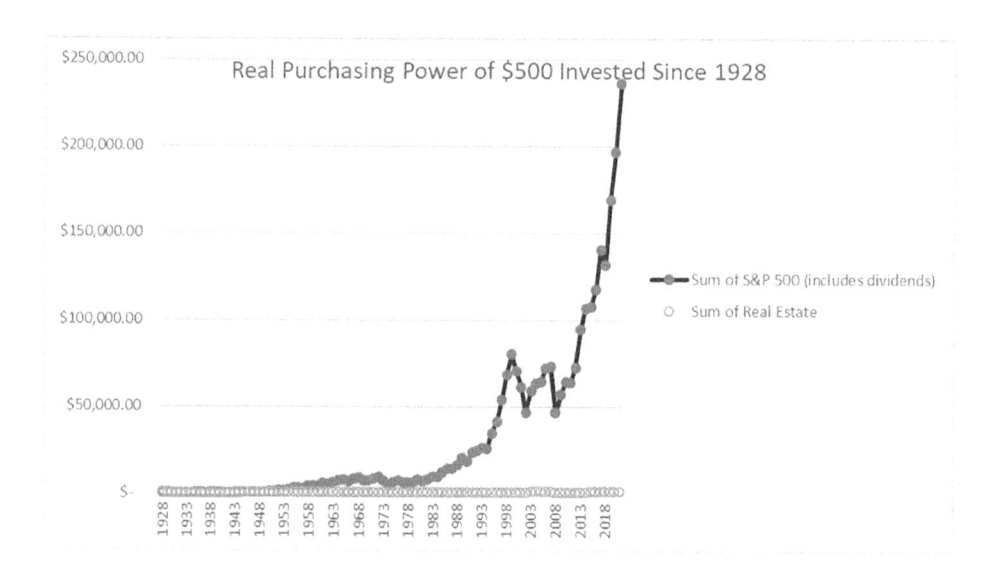

Real Purchasing Power of $500 Invested Since 1928

	1938	1948	1958	1968	1978	1988	1998	2008	2018	2021
S&P 500	$750.89	$824.77	$4,297.58	$9,001.43	$6,492.96	$16,275.22	$68,393.74	$46,507.21	$131,823.26	$236,405.89
Real Estate	$551.10	$689.30	$775.29	$731.39	$831.65	$901.17	$835.77	$1,075.11	$1,207.79	$1,455.39

On paper, your initial $500 investment in the S&P 500 would still be $3,808,554.17 in 2021. The same $500 investment in real estate is $23,446.74 at the end of 2021. However, the purchasing power of money has declined, and in 2021, $3,808,554.17 would only be able to buy $236,405.89 worth of goods from 1928. With the money from real estate investments, the $23,446.74 in 2021 would have declined to $1,455.39 in real dollar value. It is really important to have investments that can substantially outpace the rate of inflation. From 1928 to 2021, the average rate of inflation is 3.08% per year.

Stocks versus Gold

When inflation starts to rise, people are immediately sent into a panic. People say that the best way to protect against inflation is to store your money in gold as it is a good store of value. Are gold investments really the best way to protect my portfolio from inflation? I knew that gold would hold its value during bouts of inflation, but would the safety and the returns provided from gold be commensurate with the returns of the S&P 500?

I have gathered data on the average gold and S&P 500 returns from 1969. I have put the table in the appendix, but to make it easier to see the long-term trends, I created a chart that shows the returns of the S&P 500 compared to gold. I also added two trend lines to make the long-term trends apparent.

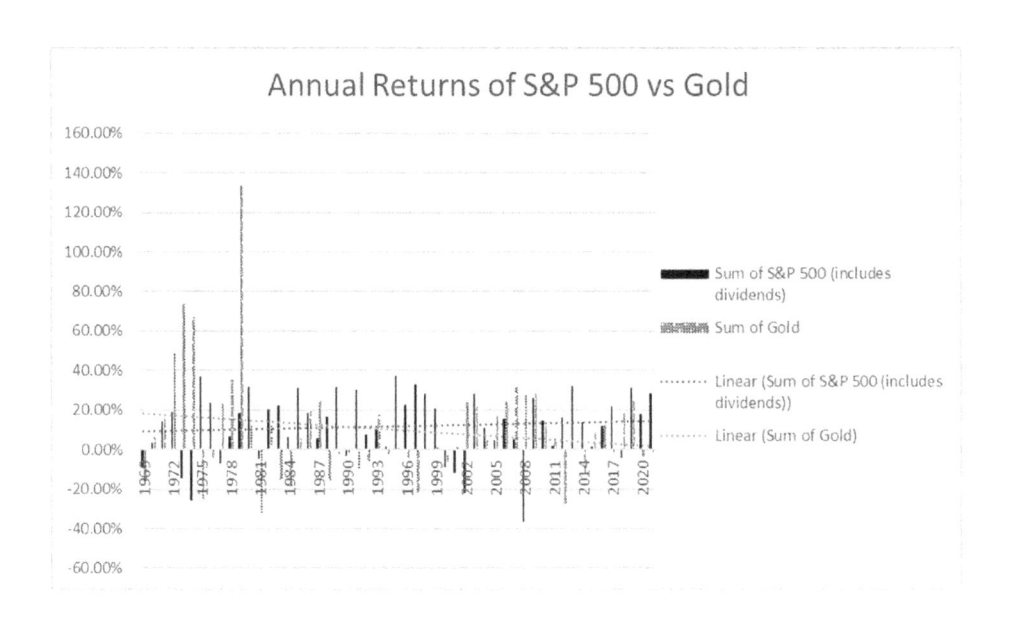

S&P 500 1970–1979 avg	7.52%	Gold 1970–1979 avg	37.46%
S&P 500 1980–1989 avg	17.95%	Gold 1980–1989 avg	-0.96%
S&P 500 1990–1999 avg	18.82%	Gold 1990–1999 avg	-2.72%
S&P 500 2000–2009 avg	1.16%	Gold 2000–2009 avg	17.38%
S&P 500 2010–2019 avg	14.02%	Gold 2010–2019 avg	4.11%

S&P 500 1969–2021 max	37.20%	Gold 1969–2021 max	133.41%
S&P 500 1969–2021 min	-36.55%	Gold 1929–2021 min	-32.15%
S&P 500 1969–2021 avg	11.94%	Gold 1969–2021 avg	10.04%
S&P 500 1969–2021 standard deviation	16.75%	Gold 1969–2021 standard deviation	27.26%

The solid black bars are the returns of the S&P 500, and the dotted bars are for the returns for gold investments. There are trendlines for both asset classes. The maximum return in the S&P 500 during the years between 1969–2021 was 37.2%, but the maximum return for gold investments during the same time period was 133.41%. The minimum return in the S&P 500 during the years between 1969–2021 was -36.55%, but the minimum return for gold investments during the same time period was slightly better at -32.15% The average return in the S&P 500 from 1969 to 2021 is 11.94%, opposed to gold with an average return of 10.04%. As you can see from the table, every decade did not produce the average return. Every year varied and was either higher or lower than average. Thus, I calculated the standard deviation to see the average variance among asset classes. The standard deviation of the S&P 500 is 16.75%, opposed to gold investments with a standard deviation of 27.26%. In three of the five decades from 1970–2019, the S&P 500 produced a higher average return than gold investments.

If you were to invest $500 in the S&P 500 or gold in 1969 and held until 2021, your returns would be as follows:

SO YOU WANT TO BE A SUPERINVESTOR?

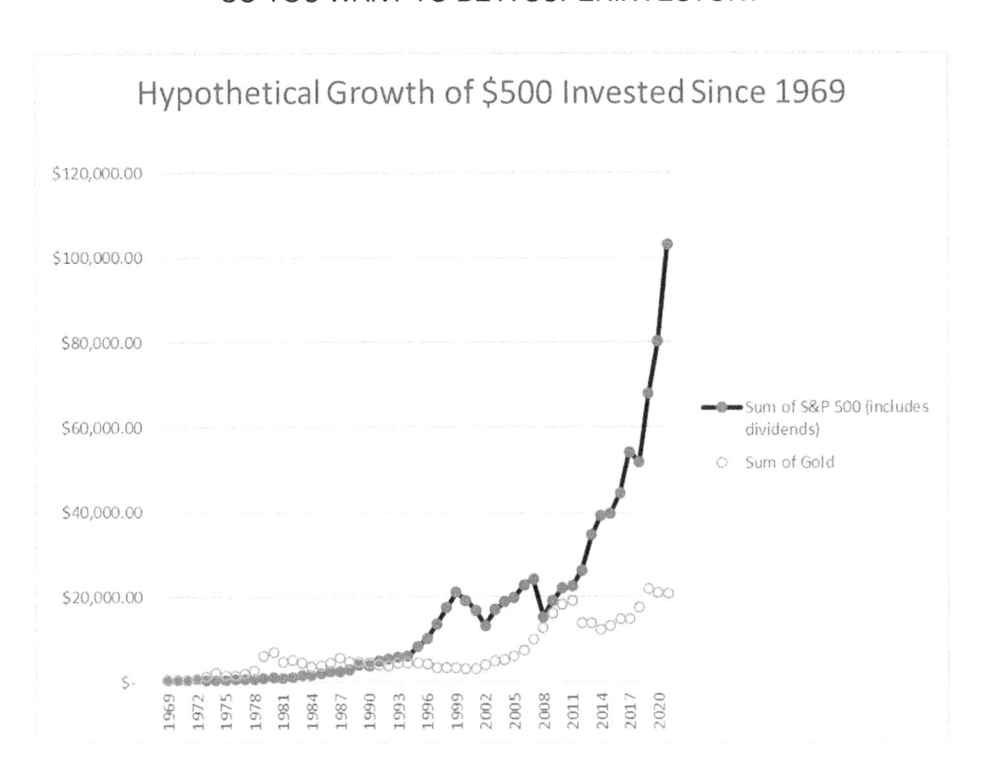

Hypothetical Growth of $500 Invested Since 1969

	1969	1979	1989	1999	2009	2019	2021
S&P 500	$458.79	$815.17	$4,034.48	$21,203.08	$19,265.84	$67,994.07	$103,094.68
Gold	$419.65	$6,245.74	$4,780.37	$3,467.32	$16,257.53	$21,846.37	$20,843.47

Initially the value of $500 in either asset class was the same. By 1979, gold prices jumped and then came back to around the same value as the S&P 500 in 1989. Around 1995, the two asset classes diverged just to come back to the same value around 2007. From 2007 to 2021, the S&P 500 had much higher annual returns than gold, and money was compounded at a higher rate. The initial $500 investment in the S&P 500 has grown to $103,094.68 in 2021, but that same $500 investment in gold only grew to $20,843.47 by 2021. Around 2009, the federal government stepped in and began quantitative easing began, and we saw outsized returns in the stock market compared to gold assets.

Unfortunately, inflation still diminishes the real returns of our investment.

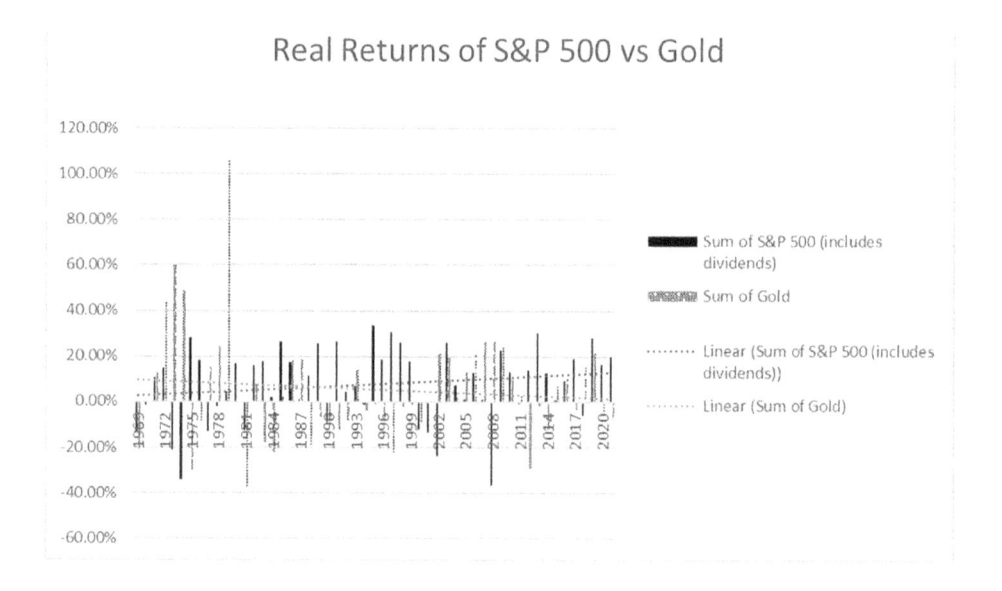

Real Returns of S&P 500 vs Gold

S&P 500 1970–1979 avg	0.40%	Gold 1970–1979 avg	27.25%
S&P 500 1980–1989 avg	12.27%	Gold 1980–1989 avg	-5.63%
S&P 500 1990–1999 avg	15.53%	Gold 1990–1999 avg	-5.49%
S&P 500 2000–2009 avg	-1.43%	Gold 2000–2009 avg	14.52%
S&P 500 2010–2019 avg	12.06%	Gold 2010–2019 avg	2.29%
S&P 500 1969–2021 max	33.80%	Gold 1969–2021 max	106.02%
S&P 500 1969–2021 min	-36.61%	Gold 1929–2021 min	-37.71%
S&P 500 1969–2021 avg	7.76%	Gold 1969–2021 avg	5.58%
S&P 500 1969–2021 standard deviation	16.63%	Gold 1969–2021 standard deviation	24.03%

We still see the same long-term trend in the S&P 500 and gold investments as the annual returns are impacted the same way for both asset classes. The maximum return in the S&P 500 during the years between 1969–2021 was 33.8%, but the maximum return for gold investments during the same time period was 106.02%. The minimum return in the S&P 500 during the years between 1969–2021 was -36.61%, but the minimum return for gold investments during the same time period was slightly worse at -37.71%. The average return in the S&P 500 from 1969 to 2021 is 7.76%, opposed to gold with an average return of 5.58%. As you can see from the table, every decade did not produce the average return. Every year varied and was either higher or lower than average. Thus, I calculated the standard deviation to see the average variance among asset classes. The standard deviation of the S&P 500 is 16.63% from 1969 to 2021, opposed to gold investments with a standard deviation of 24.03%. In three of the five decades from 1970 to 2019, the S&P 500 produced a higher average return than gold investments.

Once we begin compounding the inflation rate over time, we see a major difference.

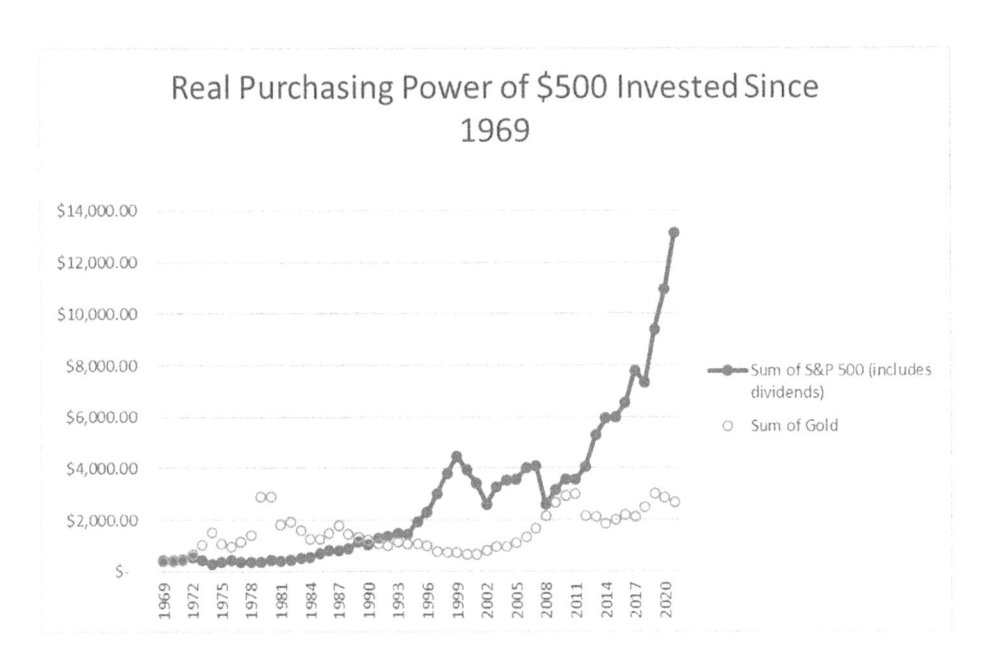

Real Purchasing Power of $500 Invested Since 1969

	1969	1979	1989	1999	2009	2019	2021
S&P 500	$432.02	$377.30	$1,135.80	$4,472.43	$3,167.13	$9,393.13	$13,131.57
Gold	$395.16	$2,890.79	$1,345.78	$731.37	$2,672.59	$3,018.00	$2,654.91

On paper, your initial $500 investment in the S&P 500 is $103,094.68 in 2021, and that same $500 investment in gold only grew to $20,843.47 by 2021. However, the purchasing power of money has declined and the $103,094.68 obtained from the S&P 500 in 2021 would only be able to buy $13,131.57 worth of goods from 1969. The $20,843.47 acquired from gold investments in 2021 would have declined to $2,654.91 in real value. For both assets, there is a roughly 87% decline from paper value to real purchasing power showing that gold investments are not a better store of value over stocks.

Stocks versus Safety Plays

Many risk-averse people have told me stocks are way too risky of an investment, and I should buy bonds for guaranteed income instead. In most cases, a bond pays fixed interest payments semi-annually to the bond holder over the life of the security. Even if the stock market is down, the bond will pay the interest to the bondholder. The only risk of holding a bond is the corporate or government entity filing for bankruptcy and not paying interest at all. Most advisors say the older you get, the more bonds you should hold as it is safer than equities. During late 2021 and most of 2022, I have seen rising rates and inflation effect stocks and bonds negatively, so I wanted to determine if the supposed less risk of bonds outweighed the returns of equities over a long period of time.

I have gathered data on three "safety plays" and S&P 500 returns from 1928. I used average returns of Baa (medium safety) corporate bonds, short-term US T-Bills, and US T-bonds. Also, I have put the yearly returns in a table in the appendix.

SO YOU WANT TO BE A SUPERINVESTOR?

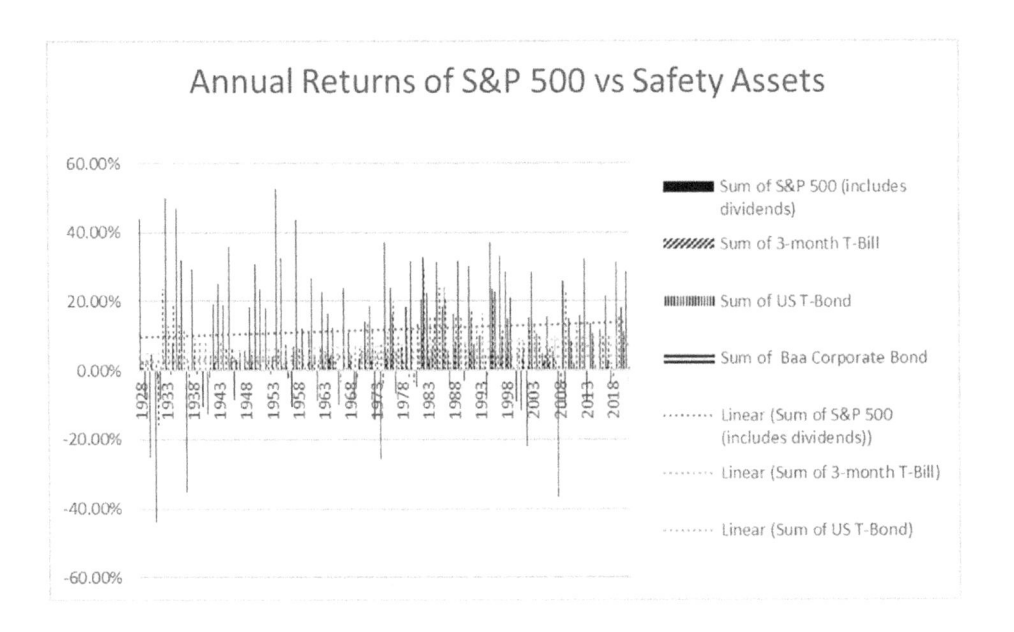

Annual Returns of S&P 500 vs Safety Assets

S&P 500 1930–1939 avg	4.27%	3-month T-billl 1930–1939 avg	0.99%
S&P 500 1940–1949 avg	9.64%	3-month T-billl 1940–1949 avg	0.48%
S&P 500 1950–1959 avg	20.93%	3-month T-billl 1950–1959 avg	2.00%
S&P 500 1960–1969 avg	8.60%	3-month T-billl 1960–1969 avg	3.98%
S&P 500 1970–1979 avg	7.52%	3-month T-billl 1970–1979 avg	6.29%
S&P 500 1980–1989 avg	17.95%	3-month T-billl 1980–1989 avg	8.82%
S&P 500 1990–1999 avg	18.82%	3-month T-billl 1990–1999 avg	4.85%
S&P 500 2000–2009 avg	1.16%	3-month T-billl 2000–2009 avg	2.69%
S&P 500 2010–2019 avg	14.02%	3-month T-billl 2010–2019 avg	0.52%
S&P 500 1928–2021 max	52.56%	3-month T-billl 1928–2021 max	14.03%
S&P 500 1928–2021 min	-43.84%	3-month T-billl 1928–2021 min	0.03%
S&P 500 1928–2021 avg	11.82%	3-month T-billl 1928–2021 avg	3.33%
S&P 500 1928–2021 standard deviation	19.46%	3-month T-billl 1928–2021 standard deviation	3.04%
US T-bond 1930–1939 avg	4.01%	Baa Corporate Bond 1930–1939 avg	7.77%
US T-bond 1940–1949 avg	2.52%	Baa Corporate Bond 1940–1949 avg	5.18%
US T-bond 1950–1959 avg	0.83%	Baa Corporate Bond 1950–1959 avg	2.32%
US T-bond 1960–1969 avg	2.51%	Baa Corporate Bond 1960–1969 avg	3.23%

US T-bond 1970–1979 avg	5.58%	Baa Corporate Bond 1970–1979 avg	7.29%
US T-bond 1980–1989 avg	12.59%	Baa Corporate Bond 1980–1989 avg	14.46%
US T-bond 1990–1999 avg	7.83%	Baa Corporate Bond 1990–1999 avg	9.69%
US T-bond 2000–2009 avg	6.62%	Baa Corporate Bond 2000–2009 avg	8.61%
US T-bond 2010–2019 avg	4.35%	Baa Corporate Bond 2010–2019 avg	7.23%
US T-bond 1928–2021 max	32.81%	Baa Corporate Bond 1928–2021 max	29.05%
US T-bond 1928–2021 min	-11.12%	Baa Corporate Bond 1928–2021 min	-15.68%
US T-bond 1928–2021 avg	5.11%	Baa Corporate Bond 1928–2021 avg	7.19%
US T-bond 1928–2021 standard deviation	7.68%	Baa Corporate Bond 1928–2021 standard deviation	7.51%

The solid black bars are the returns of the S&P 500, the diagonal striped bars are the returns for the US short term three-month T-Bill, the vertical lined bars are for the long-term US T-bond, and the horizontal lined bars are for the returns for Baa corporate bonds. There are trendlines for all the bars. The maximum return in the S&P 500 during the years between 1928–2021 was 52.56%, but the maximum return for the US T-bond was 32.81%, followed by Baa corporate bonds at 29.05%, and lastly 14.03% for three-month T-Bills. The minimum return in the S&P 500 during the years between 1928–2021 was -43.84%, but the minimum return for return for the US T-Bill was 0.03%, followed by US T-bonds at -11.12%, and lastly -15.68% for Baa corporate bonds. The average return in the S&P 500 from 1928 to 2021 is 11.82%, opposed to Baa corporate bonds at 7.19%, followed by US T-bonds at 5.11%, and lastly 3.33% for three-month T-Bills. As you can see from the table, every decade did not produce the average return. Every year varied and was either higher or lower than average. Thus, I calculated the standard deviation to see the average variance among asset classes. The standard deviation of the S&P 500 is 19.46%, opposed

SO YOU WANT TO BE A SUPERINVESTOR?

to the US T-bond with a standard deviation of 7.68%, followed by Baa corporate bonds at 7.51%, and lastly 3.04% for three-month T-Bills. In seven of the nine decades from 1930 to 2019, the S&P 500 produced a higher average return than the other three assets. Baa corporate bonds were the best performing asset class in the two other decades.

If you were to invest $500 in the S&P 500 or any of the safety plays in 1928 and held until 2021, your returns would be as follows:

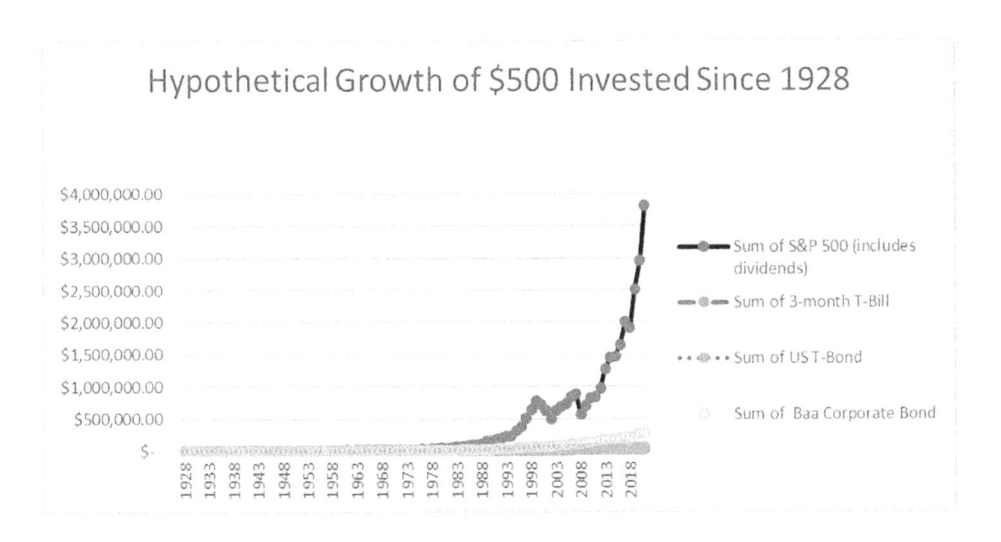

Hypothetical Growth of $500 Invested Since 1928

	1938	1948	1958	1968	1978	1988	1998	2008	2018	2021
S&P 500	$607.66	$1,148.96	$7,179.20	$18,471.15	$25,408.84	$113,362.01	$647,961.26	$565,151.11	$1,914,354.69	$3,808,554.17
3-month T-Bill	$585.91	$608.04	$724.76	$1,037.46	$1,848.54	$4,371.76	$7,249.71	$9,865.81	$10,240.98	$10,415.32
US T-Bond	$742.13	$947.90	$1,101.94	$1,435.55	$1,390.03	$6,073.91	$15,874.73	$30,065.52	$36,543.27	$42,634.75
Baa Corporate Bond	$985.26	$1,668.95	$2,170.57	$3,076.81	$6,084.90	$19,208.12	$54,503.40	$99,725.11	$210,999.30	$271,188.22

Initially the value of $500 in all the asset classes were the same. Around 1958, the S&P 500 diverged from the other asset classes. From 1958 to 2021, the S&P 500 had much higher annual returns than bonds, and money was compounded at a higher rate. The initial $500 investment in the S&P 500 has grown to $3,808,554.17 by 2021, the investment in T-Bills is $10,415.32, the investments in T-bonds has grown to $42,634.75. The Baa corporate bond investment grew to $271,188.22 by 2021.

Unfortunately, inflation still diminishes the real returns of our investment.

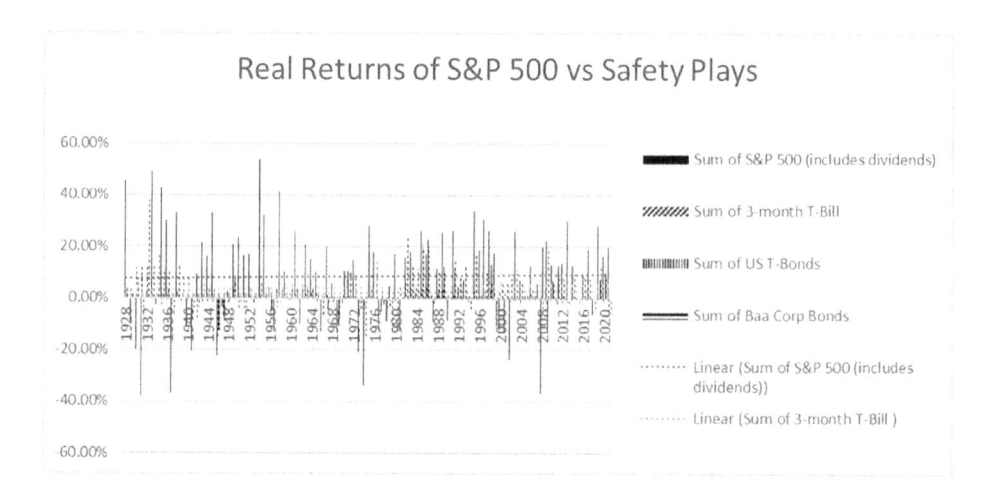

Real Returns of S&P 500 vs Safety Plays

S&P 500 1930–1939 avg	5.72%	3-month T-billl 1930–1939 avg	3.26%
S&P 500 1940–1949 avg	4.56%	3-month T-billl 1940–1949 avg	-4.50%
S&P 500 1950–1959 avg	18.40%	3-month T-billl 1950–1959 avg	-0.20%
S&P 500 1960–1969 avg	6.04%	3-month T-billl 1960–1969 avg	1.42%
S&P 500 1970–1979 avg	0.40%	3-month T-billl 1970–1979 avg	-0.99%
S&P 500 1980–1989 avg	12.27%	3-month T-billl 1980–1989 avg	3.54%
S&P 500 1990–1999 avg	15.53%	3-month T-billl 1990–1999 avg	1.87%
S&P 500 2000–2009 avg	-1.43%	3-month T-billl 2000–2009 avg	0.16%
S&P 500 2010–2019 avg	12.06%	3-month T-billl 2010–2019 avg	-1.22%
S&P 500 1928–2021 max	53.71%	3-month T-billl 1928–2021 max	12.82%
S&P 500 1928–2021 min	-38.07%	3-month T-billl 1928–2021 min	-15.03%
S&P 500 1928–2021 avg	8.60%	3-month T-billl 1928–2021 avg	0.35%
S&P 500 1928–2021 standard deviation	19.34%	3-month T-billl 1928–2021 standard deviation	3.83%
US T-bond 1930–1939 avg	6.29%	Baa Corporate Bond 1930–1939 avg	10.04%

US T-bond 1940–1949 avg	-2.52%	Baa Corporate Bond 1940–1949 avg	0.04%
US T-bond 1950–1959 avg	-1.33%	Baa Corporate Bond 1950–1959 avg	0.14%
US T-bond 1960–1969 avg	0.05%	Baa Corporate Bond 1960–1969 avg	0.75%
US T-bond 1970–1979 avg	-1.52%	Baa Corporate Bond 1970–1979 avg	0.15%
US T-bond 1980–1989 avg	7.35%	Baa Corporate Bond 1980–1989 avg	9.13%
US T-bond 1990–1999 avg	4.78%	Baa Corporate Bond 1990–1999 avg	6.58%
US T-bond 2000–2009 avg	4.03%	Baa Corporate Bond 2000–2009 avg	5.92%
US T-bond 2010–2019 avg	2.54%	Baa Corporate Bond 2010–2019 avg	5.37%
US T-bond 1928–2021 max	27.92%	Baa Corporate Bond 1928–2021 max	37.74%
US T-bond 1928–2021 min	-13.78%	Baa Corporate Bond 1928–2021 min	-14.88%
US T-bond 1928–2021 avg	2.14%	Baa Corporate Bond 1928–2021 avg	4.16%
US T-bond 1928–2021 standard deviation	8.64%	Baa Corporate Bond 1928–2021 standard deviation	8.66%

We still see the same long-term trends in the S&P 500 and the safer bond plays as the annual returns are impacted the same way for all asset classes. The maximum return in the S&P 500 during the years between 1928–2021 was 53.71%, but the maximum return for the Baa corporate bond was 37.74%, followed by US T-bonds at 27.92%, and lastly 12.82% for three-month T-Bills. The minimum return in the S&P 500 during the years between 1928–2021 was -38.07%, but the minimum return for the US T-bonds was -13.78%, followed by Baa corporate bonds at -14.88%, and lastly -15.03% for US T-bills. The average return in the S&P 500 from 1928 to 2021 is 8.6%, opposed to Baa corporate bonds at 4.16%, followed by US T-bonds at 2.14%, and lastly 0.35% for three-month T-Bills. As you can see from the table, every decade did not produce the average return. Every year varied and was either higher or lower than average. Thus, I calculated the standard deviation to see the average variance among asset classes. The standard deviation of the S&P 500 is 19.34%, opposed to the Baa corporate bond with a standard deviation of 8.66%, followed by US T-bonds at 8.64%, and lastly 3.83% for three-month T-Bills. In seven of the nine decades from 1930 to 2019, the S&P 500 produced a higher average return than the other three assets. Baa corporate bonds were the best performing asset class in the two other decades. Once we begin compounding the inflation rate over time, we see the major difference.

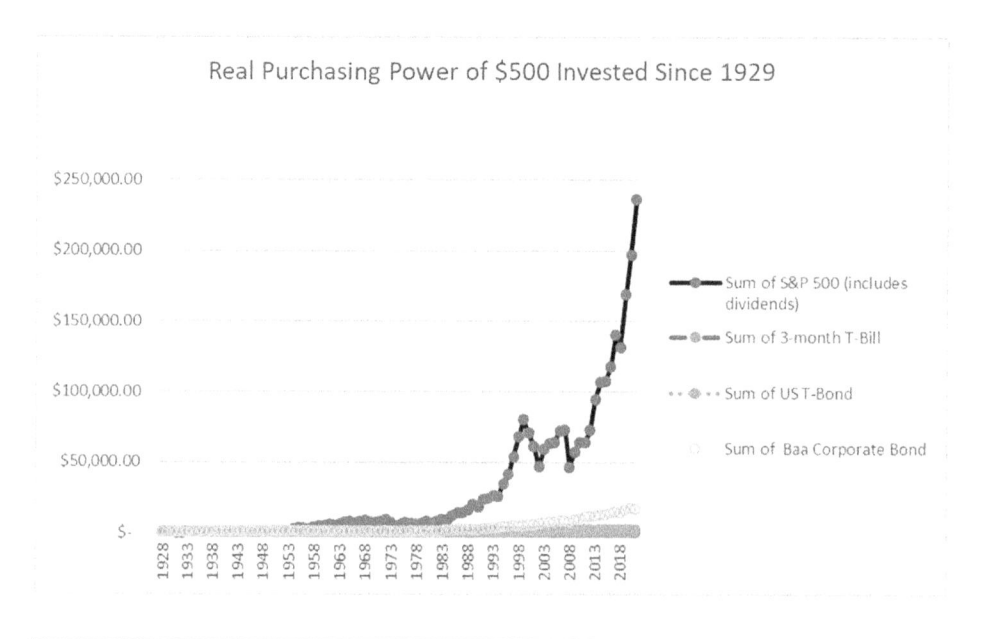

Real Purchasing Power of $500 Invested Since 1929

	1938	1948	1958	1968	1978	1988	1998	2008	2018	2021
S&P 500	$750.89	$824.77	$4,297.58	$9,001.43	$6,492.96	$16,275.22	$68,393.74	$46,507.21	$131,823.26	$236,405.89
3-month T-Bill	$724.02	$436.48	$433.85	$505.58	$472.37	$627.65	$765.22	$811.87	$705.20	$646.50
US T-Bond	$917.06	$680.44	$659.64	$699.58	$586.34	$872.02	$1,675.61	$2,474.14	$2,516.38	$2,646.44
Baa Corporate Bond	$1,217.50	$1,198.04	$1,299.34	$1,499.40	$1,554.93	$2,757.68	$5,752.95	$8,206.54	$14,529.50	$16,833.29

On paper, your initial $500 investment in the S&P 500 would be $3,808,554.17 in 2021, the investment in T-Bills is $10,415.32

SO YOU WANT TO BE A SUPERINVESTOR?

in 2021, and the investments in T-bonds $42,634.75 in 2021. The Baa corporate bond investment grew to $271,188.22 by 2021. However, the purchasing power of money has declined, and an S&P investment would only buy $236,405.89 worth of goods from 1928, a T-Bill investment could buy $646.50 worth of goods from 1928, T-bonds would only provide $2,646.44 worth of real value, and a Baa corporate bond could buy $16,833.29 worth of goods from 1928.

What It Looks Like from 1991

In the previous sections, I wanted to show you the long-term performance of major asset classes since data was available. Since you probably did not invest during the Great Depression, let's change the timeframe to incorporate just the last thirty years. In the last thirty years, we have seen the dot-com bust, 9/11, the 2008 housing crisis, and the 2020 pandemic that impacted the financial markets. Were stocks still the best asset class to hold during this shorter and very turbulent timeframe?

I have taken all the return data for the six main asset classes from 1991 to make the following charts.

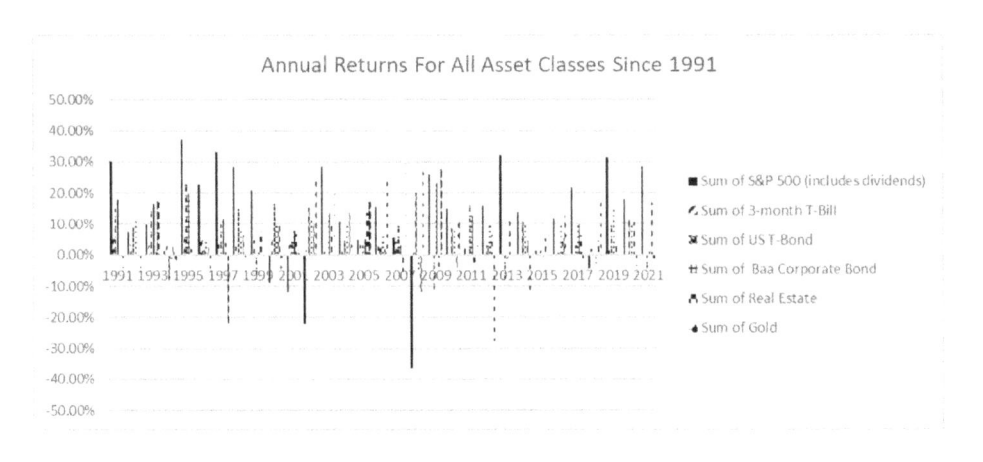

Annual Returns For All Asset Classes Since 1991

- Sum of S&P 500 (includes dividends)
- Sum of 3-month T-Bill
- Sum of US T-Bond
- Sum of Baa Corporate Bond
- Sum of Real Estate
- Sum of Gold

The solid black bars are for the returns of the S&P 500, the diagonal striped bars are for the US short-term three-month T-Bill, the spherical bars are for the returns of the long-term US T-bond, and the grid bars are for the returns of the Baa corporate bonds. The checker board bars are for the real estate returns, and the diamond bars are for the returns of gold. The average return in the S&P 500 from 1991 to 2021 is 12.56%, 2.36% for the US T-Bill, 6.09% for the US T-bond, 8.40% for a Baa corporate bond, 4.40% for real estate investments, and 5.99% for an investment in gold. Now let's say we were to invest $500 in any of the asset classes in 1991 and held until 2021 our returns would be as follows:

Hypothetical Growth of $500 Invested in All Asset Classes Since 1991

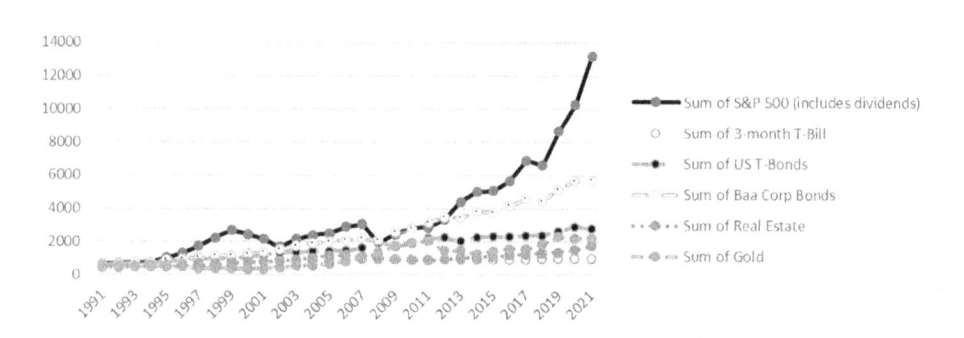

	1991	1996	2001	2006	2011	2016	2021
S&P 500	$651.17	$1,312.74	$2,173.76	$2,922.37	$2,887.54	$5,688.54	$13,180.62
3-month T-Bill	$526.88	$648.15	$816.76	$917.91	$816.76	$979.57	$1,025.02
US T-Bond	$575.02	$827.24	$1,180.93	$1,495.48	$2,214.32	$2,340.77	$2,807.00
Baa Corporate Bond	$589.27	$956.26	$1,372.27	$2,156.98	$3,177.65	$4,188.73	$5,743.90
Real Estate	$499.21	$549.49	$763.79	$1,205.94	$889.63	$1,213.97	$1,801.76
Gold	$451.90	$472.58	$353.56	$812.85	$2,057.62	$1,603.29	$2,235.78

SO YOU WANT TO BE A SUPERINVESTOR?

Initially the value of $500 invested in any of the asset classes were the same. Around 1995, the S&P 500 diverged from the other asset classes just to come back to the same levels in 2003. Our next change comes around 2007. From 2007 to 2011, the S&P 500 and Baa corporate bonds moved higher than all the other assets. After 2011, the S&P 500 provided very high returns, and money was compounded at a higher rate. The initial $500 investment in the S&P 500 has grown to $13,180.62, if you invested in T-Bills, your investment is now $1,025.02, $2,807.00 if invested in T-bonds, $5,743.90 from Baa corporate bonds; $1,801.76 from real estate investments; and $2,235.78 if invested in gold.

Unfortunately, inflation still diminishes the real returns of our investment.

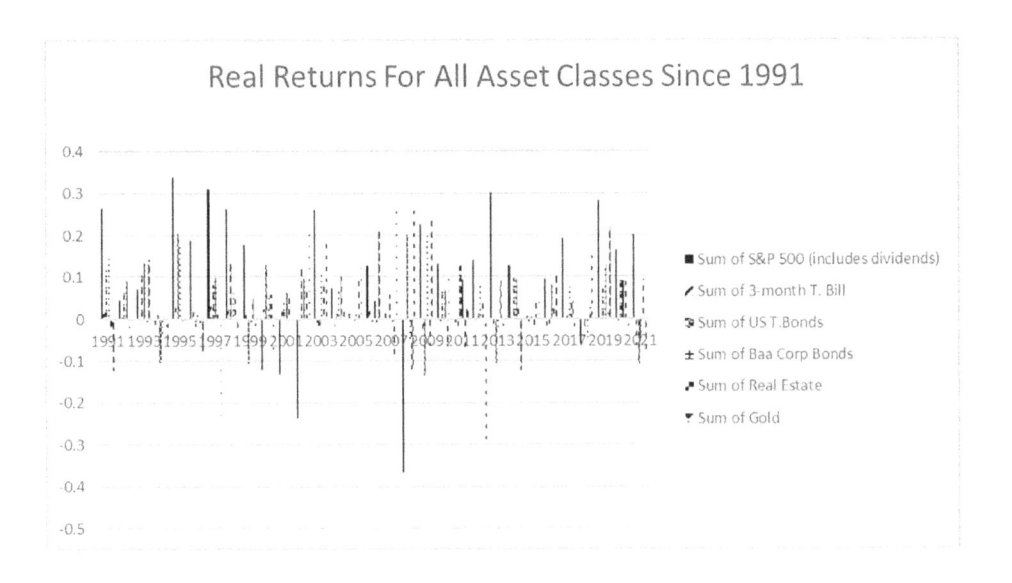

Real Returns For All Asset Classes Since 1991

- Sum of S&P 500 (includes dividends)
- Sum of 3-month T. Bill
- Sum of US T.Bonds
- Sum of Baa Corp Bonds
- Sum of Real Estate
- Sum of Gold

We still see the same long-term trends in all the asset classes as the annual returns are impacted the same way. Once we begin compounding the inflation rate over time, we see the major difference.

Real Growth of $500 Invested in All Asset Classes Since 1991

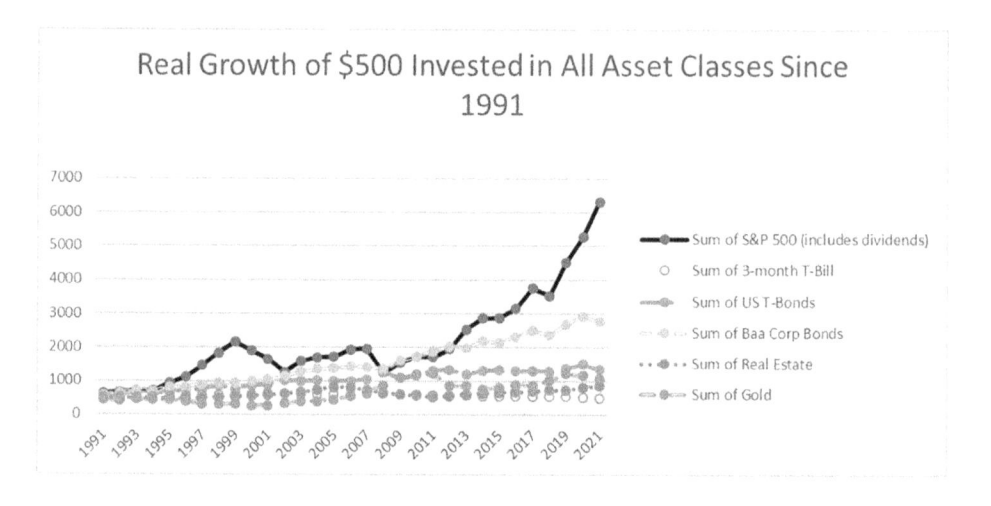

	1991	1996	2001	2006	2011	2016	2021
S&P 500	$631.81	$1,107.47	$1,646.00	$1,937.63	$1,712.01	$3,152.55	$6,327.67
3-month T-Bill	$511.21	$546.80	$618.47	$608.60	$577.62	$542.87	$492.08
US T-Bond	$557.93	$697.89	$894.22	$991.55	$1,312.86	$1,297.24	$1,347.57
Baa Corporate Bond	$571.75	$806.73	$1,039.11	$1,430.15	$1,884.02	$2,321.37	$2,757.50
Real Estate	$484.37	$463.57	$578.35	$799.58	$527.46	$672.77	$864.98
Gold	$438.46	$398.68	$267.72	$538.95	$1,219.96	$888.53	$1,073.34

On paper, your initial $500 investment in the S&P 500 would still be $13,180.62, $1,025.02 for short-term T-Bills, an investment in T-Bonds is still $2,807.00, $5,743.90 for Baa corporate bonds, $1,801.76 for real estate investments, and $2,235.78 if invested in gold. However, the purchasing power of money has declined, and an S&P investment would only buy $6,327.87 worth of goods from 1991, a T-Bill investment could buy $492.08 worth of goods, T-bonds would only buy $1,347.57 worth of goods, a Baa corporate bond $2,757.50 worth of goods, $864.98 worth of goods if invested in real estate, and $1,073.34 worth of goods from gold investments. Even if we shorten the time horizon, we see that investing in the S&P 500 provides the best returns, followed by Baa corporate bonds, then long-term T-bonds, gold, real estate, and lastly short-term T-Bills.

SO YOU WANT TO BE A SUPERINVESTOR?

The main conclusions are the following:

1. The longer you hold an asset, you will likely see much higher total returns.
2. In any given decade, one asset class may perform better than another.
3. If you are holding an investment for decades, then equity investments or investing in a market index will provide better returns than any other asset.
4. You need to find investments that can outpace the rate of inflation.

Note: These are averages. If you can find undervalued investments in any asset class, you are likely to outperform. The question then becomes what is your confidence that you can find the undervalued asset.

CHAPTER 7
You Need a Process!

Think of your favorite machine and how it works. Mine is my single serve coffee machine because I need a cup of coffee to stay awake. To use the machine, I need to fill the water tank, insert a coffee pod, select the brew size, and then hit brew. Using a better-quality pod and proper maintenance of the machine will lead to better-tasting coffee. Similarly in investing, you should follow a guide to select quality stocks for the compounding machine that will increase your chance of success. But where can you find these investments? First, you need to think about which industry do you know a lot about or want to learn about since you think the industry will produce stocks that will be great long-term holds. (I view long term holds as at least five to ten years. Many professionals who are not worried about compounding say long-term is two to three months.) Once you have identified the industry you want to research, you need to determine which specific investment(s) are worthy of your money. Now let's take a look on how to find these great stocks.

7.1 You Need to Create a Watch List!

Going back to my coffee example, my taste in coffee changes from hazelnut, caramel, and assortment packs. When I select coffee, I first have to decide what type of flavored coffee or mix of coffees do I want to buy. For this example, I chose caramel. From here, I will go on Amazon and search for all caramel coffee pods that fit into my machine. Then I eliminate all the coffee selections that are not medium roast, as I do not like light or bold roasts. From the remaining choices, I will select a few of my favorite brands that sell quality coffee. I will also read the reviews from other customers and make sure the product is highly rated. Amazon will also show a list of similar products that I will look at to see if these competing products have a better rating. Finally, I have a budget of what I am willing to pay for coffee, and if a particular box of pods is unreasonably priced, I will look for something else. Similarly much of this same selection process is used when selecting stocks. It is very daunting to open a financial website and see thousands of stocks that you have never heard of. These websites are trying to scare you on purpose so you make the decision to give your hard-earned money to a money manager who is only concerned about collecting a fee. Don't worry, there is nothing to worry about if you are reading this book. I will share with you the process that I use to select stocks.

Lifestyle Research

I always had a passion for stocks from a young age and always had a sense for good products. I used many different search engines back when I was younger that were all user unfriendly, and using the Internet was a chore. Then one search engine came along that was so easy to use, that I and all of my friends started to use this search engine and never looked back. Similarly, when starting your search for investments, look around and take notice of what items you use on a daily basis and could not live without. Find out which company makes the product or provides the service. Then ask yourself two questions: first, do others use or need the product, and second, do you know or want to know more about the industry and company? You can also start by doing "scuttlebutt" research, a term coined by Phil Fisher to do research on a company by talking to others to see how they feel about a company. Now let's move on to see how we can use media information in our search for stocks.

Media Research

I want to discuss three useful points on how you can use the media to help narrow down your stock search. First, listen to what industries are constantly being talked about and avoided in the news, the financial media, dinner parties, or among friends. In both cases, you can find industries with investments that can be diamonds in the rough. If everyone is talking about a particular industry, inevitably their ego takes over, and they boast how great of an investment they made. Then everyone else exclaims they can do that too. This is how bubbles start. I like to stay away from these high-flying names, but I am also aware that well-established names or other players with steady growth and likelihood of surviving fifteen to twenty years in that industry are undervalued because everyone is pouring money into stocks that will make them millionaires overnight. On the other hand, industries that are not being talked about have many investments that are undervalued. When momentum shifts from high-flying industries to safer plays, the influx of cash will boost the price of these "boring" industries and hopefully your specific investment too.

Second, we need to be honest with ourselves and determine which industries do we have experience with or are capable of understanding if we do the research. Don't worry, you do not need to understand every industry to make money. Warren Buffett stayed away from technology for the longest time since he did not understand the industry (he recently bought Apple because he saw the eye-popping ROE and ROIC numbers), and he made tons of money prior to investing in technology. If you can understand a few industries to find undervalued stocks, you will make a lot of money.

Lastly, let's take a look at the mutual and exchange traded funds in that industry. These industry funds are comprised of a group of stocks that meet an investing goal. On any financial website, you can find the performance of the funds relative to the market index (Dow Jones, Nasdaq, or S&P 500). Select only funds that are beating the market, and view the top stock holdings of the fund. I tend to select a few names that are repeated across many of the funds with a high weightage to research. You also want to research other top names that do not have a high weightage because they might be preforming better than some of the highest weightage stocks. I also want a few of the "bad stocks" in the fund so I can differentiate between the winners and losers in the industry. Now the fun begins!

7.2 You Need to Understand the Current and Future Business!

Identify the Value Chain

When I was around four years old, I used to watch the 7:00 p.m. financial news with my dad. I would say that IBM went down two points or Microsoft went up two points. I thought this was an arcade with a pinball machine for adults. I had no idea what was going on or what was the stock market.

Now that I have begun to research the stock market, I have learned what a stock actually is. **A stock is not a piece of paper; it is your proportional share of the business.** If the business makes a profit, then you receive a proportional share of the profits. On the other hand, if the business is losing money and not growing, eventually you will lose money too. Thus, it is crucial to understand how the business makes money and what is the value the business provides.

While reading up on a company, some questions to keep in mind are, What are the costs to produce and sell the product or service? What is the entire sales process—from order to fulfillment? What is the cost of keeping the business operating not including production costs (marketing, research and development, administrative and other operating expenses)? How effective are the company's research and development efforts in relation to its size? Sometimes a growth company will show a loss in earnings, but most of the money is being spent on R&D efforts for profits in the future. For example, initially Amazon was unprofitable for years; however, there were many R&D expenditures that contributed to Amazon becoming a $3,000 stock. Does the company have an above average sales organization? What is the company doing to maintain or improve profit margins? Since we want to hold the company's stock for many years, we need to think about events that will happen in the future and if the company will survive these events. Since inflation increases a company's expenses and competitors will pressure profit margins, you should pay attention to a company's strategy for reducing costs and improving profit margins over the long haul. I do not expect you to answer every question listed above, but I want to make you think before investing. Getting the right mindset before investing can go a long way.

Growth

No matter how well a stock preformed in the past, you can only buy at the present moment and hold the stock for the future. The toughest part about investing is trying to figure out what the future will hold. We need to assess the pipeline of future products and growth initiatives the company is working on.

Ask yourself these questions: Does the company have products or services that will lead to a sizable increase in sales for at least several years? What conditions have produced prior results and will those conditions be present in the future? Does the firm have the ability to enter new markets and compete against established players in those markets? When the company enters a new market does it use ingenuity or novelty to gain traction? Is there ample opportunity for this company to grow from here? Does this company have plenty of room to expand in its core business areas? Is the company and its products at an early stage in its maturity cycle? If the company's products are at a late stage in their maturity cycle, are they the best offerings available? Is the industry growing? Is the growth rate of this company accelerating? Is this company growing its share of the market? Does this business have alternative business avenues to pursue? Are the company's end markets stable/shrinking/growing? Is the company susceptible to rapid (technological) change? I have seen many industry leaders become complacent and fail to innovate; this leaves the door open for competitors to enter the business and carve out a significant chunk of market share.

Is There Demand?

No matter how good the current product(s) or future growth potential of the company are, nothing really matters if customers are not receptive of the product. Remember the Zune? The Zune was a quality mp3 player launched by Microsoft to compete with the iPod. The Zune failed because most customers were comfortable with and enjoyed the ease of use of the iPod. Customers had no intention of buying the Zune. Even a great company like Microsoft was subject to the product failure due to the lack of demand. In investing, it is crucial to understand how the customer interacts with the product or service. This information can be gathered from keen observation in stores, reading product reviews on a website, or reading analyst reports.

While gathering this information, ask yourself the following questions: Are the company's products better than competitors? Does the product(s) offer a superior feature set? Are customers willing to pay up for the company's products? Is there social status assigned to this company's products? Do customers have an emotional connection to the company's products? Are the company's products more convenient? Are the company's products easier to access than its competitors'? Does this company act as the default choice for consumers? Is the company able to maintain or increase the prices of its products over time? Do customers regularly return to purchase this company's products? Is there enthusiasm surrounding this organization? Are shareholders devoted to the company? Do employees, customers, and shareholders advocate on behalf of the organization? Does this company fulfill a real customer need? Is there long-term demand for this company's products? Are customers delighted with this company's products? Do customers consciously choose this company's products over alternatives? Do customers ask for this company's products by name? Are customers' lives improved for having purchased this company's products? Is the world better off for having this company in operation? No matter how good the product is, if it sits on a shelf, it will fail, and so will your investment.

Note: Sometimes a good company, like Microsoft, can even have a product that fails. These failures may not be critical for big companies but are important to keep a lookout for potential danger.

7.3 You Need to Defend Your Investment from Competitive Forces!

I love watching most sports where there is intense competition. Investing is the ultimate competitive game. Investing is all about selecting a particular company's stock that is superior than the other competing companies. If a company is excellent in providing investors with great returns and generating high profits, it won't be long before another company tries to compete and replicate the success or do better. I know back in kindergarten, we were told to play nice in the sandbox with others, but in business, every company wants to be the best in their own space even (especially) at the expense of others. If you are putting your hard-earned money into a business, you need to be sure the business can defend your money.

Warren Buffett highlights the importance of a company being able to defend itself with his famous moat analogy and how some of his best investments have a strong moat. "A truly great business must have an enduring 'moat' that protects excellent returns on invested capital. The dynamics of capitalism guarantee that competitors will repeatedly assault any business 'castle' that is earning high returns. Therefore a formidable barrier such as a company's being the low-cost producer (GEICO, Costco) or possessing a powerful worldwide brand (Coca-Cola, Gillette, American Express) is essential for sustained success. Business history is filled with 'Roman Candles,' companies whose moats proved illusory and were soon crossed.

"Our criterion of 'enduring' causes us to rule out companies in industries prone to rapid and continuous change. Though capitalism's 'creative destruction' is highly beneficial for society, it precludes investment certainty. A moat that must be continuously rebuilt will eventually be no moat at all." (Buffett 2009).

It is very difficult to find a moat. "There's no formula that gives you that precisely, you know, that says that the moat is 28 feet wide and 16 feet deep, you know, or anything of the sort. You have to understand the businesses. And that's what drives the academics crazy, because they know how to calculate standard deviations and all kinds of things, but that doesn't tell them anything. And that what really tells you something is if you know how to figure out how wide the moat is and whether it's likely to widen further or shrink on you" (Investment Masters Class).

After taking a real-life monopoly approach to investing, I found the best way to see if the company has a very wide moat is to read the 10K, 10Q, and other SEC filings from the company or other research reports that are written about the company. Now let's look at some factors that contribute to a moat.

What Is the Industry Dynamics?

Before we get into the specifics of a company, we need to see how the company stacks up in its industry. There are many different industries, and each industry has different dynamics. Some industries like technology have high growth, but other industries like utilities are more stable and provide a steady dividend with minimal growth.

When researching an industry, some questions to ask yourself are the following: Is the business a major player in the industry? What is the secret sauce that makes the products unique? Can the business compete to thrive or dominate in the industry? Are there many other relevant players in the industry? Is it hard to enter into the industry? Hopefully the business you selected is a key player or leader in the industry; if it is not, then there are other companies worth researching further.

Moat

We have selected a company that is currently a key player in the industry, but what will allow the company to still be a key player in the future? Well, the company needs to have a wide moat that can help protect your investment. Here are the six keys that I look for to find an indefensible moat: brand, regulations or other barriers to entry, switching cost, network effects, price, hidden champions.

The Company Has a Strong Brand

What is your favorite brand, and why? Mine is Coke because it has been in existence from 1866 and has dominated the beverage industry. Since its inception in 1866, aside from tweaks to perfect the formula, Coke has delivered a consistent product. Coke is also a worldwide brand, meaning wherever you are in the world, if you ask for a Coke, everyone knows which beverage you are referring too. Most people don't even say do you want a cola; they just say do you want a Coke. When I go to the market to buy soda, there is the store-brand cola that is cheaper, but I will buy the branded Coke as I trust I am getting a quality product. Coke also does a good job to illicit strong feelings with their brand, and many people will not drink a competitor product because of brand loyalty. Any company that has captured "mind share" with the consumer has a strong brand moat.

Are Their Barriers to Entry?

It is common to see in the pharmaceutical industry companies protecting their products with a patent. If a specific company has patent protection, that means for a certain period of time, another company cannot come in and make a generic drug to take away profits. Other companies in the oil and gas industry may have a geographic moat and may be the only company allowed to drill in a specific area. Drilling companies have to take zoning permits and abide by many regulations, which makes it difficult for new competitors to come into the same area and open for business. Anything that makes it harder for competitors to enter or directly compete is an example of a barrier to entry moat.

It Costs a Lot to Switch

I do not think I will ever use another phone that is not an iPhone. If you have an iPhone and a MacBook or any other Apple product, you know exactly why I would not switch. The ease of use and the functionality of receiving texts and FaceTime calls on any device, and the fact that these devices are almost virus proof are the main reasons not to switch to a competitor. I, like many other people, will pay a premium for the next iPhone rather than settle for a cheaper and hard to use alternative phone. On the other hand, businesses use Microsoft over Apple as they have set up most systems with Microsoft, and it simply costs too much to redo the network and switch. In both cases, Apple and Microsoft have tremendous switching costs in a financial sense or by saving time.

The Company Enjoys Network Effects

Why do some social media companies fail and others thrive? Myspace was the most prominent social media player for some time until Facebook burst onto the scene and destroyed Myspace. What happened? We see the phenomenon of network effects in action. People saw the new features on Facebook and started switching to this new and cool platform. Eventually all of your friends were leaving Myspace and joining Facebook. To interact with friends, you too had to leave Myspace and join Facebook. The more likely a group of people are to use a product, the company will enjoy higher profits as a result of network effects.

Price Moat

I always go to Costco and load up on the essentials at a very fair price. I always wondered how is Costco able to offer low prices on big bags of produce? Since Costco can capitalize on the economies of scale or pay lower prices when items are purchased from suppliers in bulk, they can offer lower prices to the consumer. Smaller companies cannot capitalize on the economies of scale and are soon put out of business as they cannot compete with a giant like Costco on price. Being the low-cost provider of certain products gives companies a price moat.

Hidden Champions

While I was reading Peter Thiel's book *Zero to One*, the point about hidden champions really stood out to me. Hidden champions operate primarily in oligopolistic markets even on a global scale, and these companies face only limited competition (Thiel and Masters 2015).

Apple has this characteristic as Apple is in a highly competitive industry, but Apple faces mild competition from a very few competitors. The best way to protect against competition is to avoid the competition altogether by being so great that the competition cannot even reach the greatness of the business.

Most companies have a few moats, but if a company has all six moats, then that is definitely a great company. However, these moats will protect from outside attacks, but a bad management can derail any company from the inside.

7.4 You Need a Capable Operator of the Investment Machine!

My favorite coffee machine works since I follow the instructions of adding water to the reservoir tank, inserting the coffee pod, selecting the brew size, and then pressing brew. The machine would not brew coffee if there is no water in the tank or if I do not insert any type of ground coffee into the machine. Similarly no matter how good the company is, a clueless management that cannot operate a business properly will cause the business to fail, and your hard-earned money that you invested in the business will become worthless.

If you are in the investment community as a money manager or a billionaire, you can easily meet with company board members and ask what the management is doing. People like you and I do not have this luxury. How then can we evaluate management? Luckily all publicly traded companies in the US are required to file 10Q reports quarterly and 10K reports annually with the SEC. Management will also discuss their quarterly earnings results in a call with analysts, and a transcript can be found on a website like Yahoo Finance. Remember if you own stock, you own part of the business. I ask myself, if I owned 100% of the company, would I run things differently? My high school math teacher Mrs. Cisnero always told us we need to be smart lazy and there is always an easier way to solve a problem. I incorporated this into my lifestyle and always look for an easier solution to any problem. I will work hard to automate a solution so I can press a few buttons rather than doing a long drawn-out process every day. Therefore, if I were running a business, I would need the business to be so great that my only job is to not do anything foolish to derail the business. The only two questions I need to focus on are the following:

1. What is the best way to allocate capital, whether it be through expansion, reinvesting, buying back stock, or paying out a dividend?
2. If I do invest in certain areas, will I generate better returns, or will I sell the business at a loss because of my mistake?

Not all managers have the same attitude, so we need to investigate further.

Does Management Avoid Mistakes

While you gather information, ask yourself the following questions: what are the top executives doing, and is the business strong enough so their job is, don't do something foolish like waste money? Think of Steve Jobs to the sudden change to Tim Cook taking over Apple. There was a panic and sell-off on the fear of the unknown (I sold in fear too as my worst mistake), but Apple was so strong that the business rebounded and then excelled because of the rational decisions made by Tim Cook. Tim Cook is great in reinvesting and expanding into high growth areas of the market, and there is excess cash remaining that a small dividend can be paid out to shareholders. Not all managers are great like Tim Cook; there are others who have made horrible decisions and ran their company into the ground. These managers see that their business is doing so well, that they take the excess money and buy new businesses that will not help the core business in any way, and in a few years, the new business arm is sold for pennies on the dollar.

Motivation

If you are working while receiving an enormous salary and that pay is not based on your performance, what is your motivation to go above and beyond? Not much if you are able to pay all your expenses and afford luxuries. If people in management are getting a fixed multimillion-dollar salary no matter how poorly they perform, why should you expect that the executive is motivated to grow your money that you invested in the company? If management is compensated based on stock appreciation (be careful of the fraudulent manager that reports higher earnings to make the stock move higher), equity options, or returns to shareholders, then they are motivated to work in the shareholders' best interest. If you go to a financial website like Morningstar, you can find the return on equity (ROE) and return on invested capital (ROIC). Both of these numbers show if management is effective in growing your money. Later on, I will show you how the ROE and ROIC numbers are calculated. But for now, if we see both numbers in the 15–20% range, we have found a gold mine.

Is Management Rational

In my view, the main reason for a business to be in operation is to generate cash. From this cash, all the workers, rent, and other expenses are paid. What should a business do with the excess cash? A company has three options: **(1) reinvest into the business, (2) it can buy growth, or (3) it can return the money to shareholders**. In his 1987 letter to shareholders, Warren Buffet States, "The lack of skill that many CEOs have at capital allocation is no small matter: After ten years on the job, a CEO whose company annually retains earnings equal to 10% of net worth will have been responsible for the deployment of more than 60% of all the capital at work in the business.

"CEOs who recognize their lack of capital-allocation skills (which not all do) will often try to compensate by turning to their staffs, management consultants, or investment bankers. Charlie and I have frequently observed the consequences of such 'help.' On balance, we feel it is more likely to accentuate the capital-allocation problem than to solve it" (Buffett 1987).

Management needs to be able to allocate capital wisely. If management invests to look like they are doing work, but in reality, the investments are not lucrative the money should be returned to shareholders. Beware of the manager who hires outside parties to allocate capital as it rarely helps.

The Golden Goose

Have you heard the story of the Golden Goose? It is a German story where a farmer has a goose that provides him with a golden egg every day. The farmer gets greedy and impatient waiting for eggs and decides to kill the goose and get all the eggs at once. To his dismay, he finds no golden eggs inside the dead goose. The moral of the story is that you have to be patient and cannot expect to become rich overnight. Similarly, if you invest in a business and there is excess cash, is the best option to pay a dividend or to retain earnings?

Let's take a hypothetical company for our example. A business has $100 invested in it and also earns a 20% return while retaining 100% of earnings. Management could then take that $20 and reinvest it alongside the original $100 and earn a 20% return again and again and again.

1	$120.00	6	$298.60
2	$144.00	7	$358.32
3	$172.80	8	$429.98
4	$207.83	9	$515.98
5	$248.83	10	$619.17

At the end of the fourth year, you've doubled your money. At the end of ten years, you've got a six-bagger. This goes to show that if management can retain and compound the earnings at a high rate, being patient can pay off handsomely.

On the other hand, if the company retains $1 dollar and pays out a dividend from the remaining 20% of earnings, the results are as follows:

money invested	20% return	$1 retained and rest is paid as a dividend
100	120	19
101	121.2	20.2
102	122.4	21.4
103	123.6	22.6
104	124.8	23.8
105	126	25
106	127.2	26.2
107	128.4	27.4
108	129.6	28.6
109	130.8	29.8
110	132	31
Total dividend		275

It seems better that you are getting a dividend and that's cold hard cash, but you are actually interfering with the compounding effect. In this hypothetical example, allowing a company to fully retain earnings would lead to you having $619.17 after ten years. On the other hand, taking out a substantial amount in dividends one can only take out $132 from the investment and received total dividends of $275 for total of $407. That's a $212.17 difference of what one could have made by opting for a "feel good" mistake.

7.5 You Need to Look at the Financial Statements!

Harry Markopolos once said, "A decade ago, there was one energy company head and shoulders above all the others. That was Enron. There was also an insurance company above the rest. That was American International Group. In telecommunications, there was one company above all others. That was WorldCom. They were all accounting frauds.

"Today we have one company above all others in technology. That would be Apple. But there's a visible reason for that, so Apple's not a fraud. Bernie Madoff said his performance was roughly seven and half times better than the stock index he pretended to be benchmarking himself against. If you're seven times better, two things can be true: One, you're a fraud. Or two, you're an alien from outer space and have perfect foreknowledge of the capital markets" (Markopolos 2011).

If we cannot trust what all company executives say at face value, how should we get reliable information? Thankfully, the SEC requires that all publicly traded companies file quarterly 10Q and annual 10K reports. Each of these reports contain three financial statements, an income statement, a balance sheet, and a cash flow statement. Each statement gives us a valuable snapshot of how the company is actually performing. If you already have a good grasp of accounting that is great, but if you do not have an accounting background, this can be like watching paint dry. I do not like watching paint dry, so here is where my "smart lazy" kicked in. Instead of learning all the line items, I learned the key formulas, where to find the inputs on financial websites, and then let excel do all the work. The following sections are a little math intensive, but I will try to make this as painless as possible.

Income Statement

Here we have a sample income statement for a hypothetical company. The income statement begins with the revenue or sales and then goes through all the expenses of the company.

Income Statement	
Revenue	$100
Cost of goods sold	$10
Gross Income	$90
Research and Development Expense	$20
Selling, General, and Administative Expense	$5
Total Operating Expense	$25
Operating Income	$65
Interest Expense	$10
Taxes	$10
Net Income	$45

- Misleading Statements

Executives can mislead the public by saying the company had a great sales number or revenue and their top line is growing. However, as an investor looking at the income statement, the sales figure or revenue means nothing if the expenses for the cost of goods sold, operating expense, or interest expenses are high too and lower the bottom line or net income.

- Key Concept

If a company is spending on research and development (R&D), this is indicative that the company is purposely lowering the bottom line by investing in future growth. The company may experience pain today for a brighter future. Amazon did this when it was starting out, and the massive investment paid off tremendously.

- Most Important Thing

The most important number from the income statement is the net income. This important bottom line number is useful for many key calculations we will explore later.

Balance Sheet

A balance sheet answers the question, how much is the business really worth? The assets column shows us what the business owns.

Assets are financed by the bank, other businesses (liabilities), or from money invested in the business (shareholder equity). That's why we see assets on one side and the money owed or liabilities to other businesses and equity belonging to shareholders on the other side. The two sides always have to equal each other or "balance," and the fundamental balance sheet equation is Assets = Liabilities + Equity.

	Balance Sheet		
Current (Short-term) Assets	$50	Current (Short-term) liabilities	$50
Non-Current (Long-term) Assets	$250	Non-Current (Long-term) liabilities	$150
Total Assets	$300	Total Liabilities	$200
		Shareholders Equity	$100

- Misleading Statements

A great way to see how much money the company is making relative to equity is from calculating the return on equity (ROE). ROE = Net Income / Equity. As much as I think this number is very important, ROE can be easily manipulated by management taking on too much debt and making ROE artificially high.

Let's take two scenarios:

1. A company generated annual net income of $100 million with $300 million in stockholder's equity the ROE is 33% ($100/$300 = 0.33, or 33%).
2. However if annual net income was $100 million and equity is $3,000 million or 3 billion the ROE is 3.3% ($100/$3,000 = 0.033, or 3.3%).

From the ROE, it is apparent the company in example 1 is far superior. The key takeaway is the lower the equity the higher the ROE. However, return on equity does not give us the full picture of what is going on in a company. Dishonest management can manipulate this number to fool less discerning investors. To get equity in a company we use the equation Assets = Debt + Equity. Therefore, if a manager takes on too much debt, this will shrink the equity and artificially boost return on equity. Let's take a look at two hypotheticals:

1) Company A
   Net Income $600
   Assets $500
   Debt $200
   Equity $300

   ROE= net income / equity or $600/300 = 200%

2) Company B
   Net Income $600
   Assets $500
   Debt $400
   Equity $100

   ROE= net income / equity or $600/$100 = 600%

Just looking at ROE, we might assume company B is better with 600% compared to company A with 200%. However, getting into the equation, we see that company B has taken on unsustainable debt loads and has a high likelihood of failing.

- Key Concept

To get an accurate picture of the return, I like using return on invested capital (ROIC). ROIC = Net Income / Debt + Equity.

1) Company A
   Net Income $600
   Assets $500
   Debt $200
   Equity $300

   ROE= net income / equity or $600/300 = 200%

ROIC= net income / debt + equity= $600/ ($200 + $300) = 120%

2) Company B
Net Income $600
Assets $500
Debt $400
Equity $100

ROE= net income / equity or $600/$100 = 600%
ROIC= net income / debt + equity or $600/ ($400 +$100) =120%

By digging deeper, we see that the two companies produced the same returns or ROIC. By looking at the ROE relative to ROIC, we might conclude company A is better as it is taking on less debt and producing the same return as company B.

- Most Important Thing(s)

We see the effects debt can have on returns, but how would we know if the company is taking on too much debt and may face liquidity or solvency issues in the future? The first important ratio is the current ratio. This ratio determines if the company has enough current assets that can easily be turned to cash to pay off any current liabilities if there was a need for quick money.

Current ratio = current assets / current liabilities

The second ratio is the debt-to-equity ratio. The debt-to-equity ratio shows us how much leverage the company is using relative to equity. Unlike the current ratio, this formula takes into account both current and noncurrent liabilities. If the company is just taking on debt and moving it to long-term liabilities, eventually the company has to pay these obligations or it will go bankrupt. Thus, we want to use the debt-to-equity ratio to see if the company is overleveraged and will run into issue in the future.

Debt to Equity ratio = Total Liabilities / Shareholder Equity

Cash Flow Statement

The objective of any business is to make the most money as possible. Businesses are required to provide a cash flow Statement that shows how much cash is generated from operating, investing, and financing activities. I view the cash flow statement as the most important statement as it allows me to answer key questions like, where is the money going, and is the money wisely invested or spent on poor operating costs?

Cash Flow	
Net Income	$60
Depreciation and Amortization	$30
Changes in Working Capital	$10
Cash from Operating Activities	$80
Cash from Investing Activities	$0
Cash from Financing Activities	$500
Total Cash	$580

- Misleading Statements

Looking at the example above, management will say the business generated $580. This is true but does not give us the full picture. Note that cash from financing activity is $500, indicating the company sold stock or debt instruments to generate cash. A company cannot sell that much stock every quarter. This $500 raised is most likely to be from a one-time IPO and not sustainable for the future.

- Key Concept

Previously, we have seen that a positive number for cash from financing activity should be viewed as a negative. Similarly, if the cash from investing is positive, this means investments were sold to generate cash. The selling of enough investments to generate a positive cash flow is not a sustainable process and may be a one-time event. On the other hand, if cash from investing activities is negative, this indicates investments are being purchased for future growth (it is important the company invests wisely, not for the sake of getting bigger).

- Most Important Thing

Out of all the financial statements, the cash flow statement is the most important. It will allow you to answer the question, where is the money coming from? Do a thorough analysis to see what is the main source of cash coming from either from operations, selling investments, or financing activities. Remember to think through the analysis as sometimes a positive number is a bad thing.

7.6 You Need to Invert the Story!

After researching a company for a long time, it is easy to fall in love with that company's stock. As a part of human psychology, we have a confirmation bias where we will only listen to opinions confirming our findings and reject other ideas. Maybe you are right and nothing bad will happen, but you should be aware of the risks. You may never have a face-to-face encounter with a shark, but it is important to know that risk is there in the ocean. Let's see some of the tricks our brain plays and developing biases.

Mental Bias

First, we should understand the concept of the affect heuristic. The affect heuristic is the notion that people's likes and dislikes form their beliefs about a company. Once we have an opinion on the company, we tend to have a halo effect where we put the investment on a pedestal and we like or dislike everything about the company. We also have a confirmation bias, and we seek out ideas that match our beliefs and assumptions.

Instead, we should frame what we read differently. For example, if there is a 90% chance that the investment is a success, you should ask yourself, why is there a 10% chance of failure? Some other questions to ask are, What do you believe that is actually false? What the heck is my brain doing to blindside me now?

Most investors run into problems not from outside influences but from their own biases and failing to look at all of the facts. Sometimes a negative or overly positive confirmation bias can lead to very risky situations.

What Type of Risk Is It?

Pick any random day that the market declined, and watch a financial news channel for a couple of hours. Sooner or later, there will be a talking head that says the market is headed for a steep decline as the economic data doesn't support the market moving higher. They say all the signs were there to get out of the market. Well, where were these experts before the downturn? I could have sold before the downturn if someone warned me! I am reminded of Peter Lynch interview on PBS where he talks about these doomsday experts. "It's lovely to know when there's (a) recession. I don't remember anybody predicting (in) 1982 we're going to have 14 percent inflation, 12 percent unemployment, a 20 percent prime rate, you know, the worst recession since the Depression. I don't remember any of that being predicted. It just happened. It was there. It was ugly. And I don't remember anybody telling me about it. So I don't worry about any of that stuff. I've always said if you spend 13 minutes a year on economics, you've wasted 10 minutes" (Interview with Peter Lynch, PBS).

These economic forecasts are usually talking about systemic risk, like rising interest rates, inflation, or general weakness in the economy. This fear is designed to spook investors, but there is nothing you can do about these risks. If the whole market is declining, your investment is likely to decline as well by the same or greater percentage as the market. Portfolio managers try to mitigate this risk by buying derivatives as a hedge. In his 2002 letter to shareholders, Warren Buffett warns about the perils of options for casual investors. Here are some important excerpts: "I view derivatives as time bombs, both for the parties that deal in them and the economic system. Basically these instruments call for money to change hands at some future date, with the amount to be determined by one or more reference items, such as interest rates, stock prices, or currency values... One of the derivative instruments that LTCM used was total-return swaps, contracts that facilitate 100% leverage in various markets, including stocks. For example, Party A to a contract, usually a bank, puts up all of the money for the purchase of a stock while Party B, without putting up any capital, agrees that at a future date it will receive any gain or pay any loss that the bank realizes. Total-return swaps of this type make a joke of margin requirements. Beyond that, other types of derivatives severely curtail the ability of regulators to curb leverage and generally get their arms around the risk profiles of banks, insurers and other financial institutions. Similarly, even experienced investors and analysts encounter major problems in analyzing the financial condition of firms that are heavily involved with derivatives contracts. In our view, however, derivatives are financial weapons of mass destruction, carrying dangers that, while now latent, are potentially lethal" (Buffett 2003). Buffett warns that by trading in options, you may be hedging the portfolio, but you are taking on massive amounts of leverage that can collapse at any moment when the economy turns sour and banks want to take back their loans.

Instead of worrying about the economy, one just has to believe things will get better. Again Peter Lynch shares his learnings from the 1982 recession. This is very relevant as there are numerous similarities seen in 2022. "1982 was a very scary period for this country. We've had nine recessions since World War II. This was the worst. 14 percent inflation. We had a 20 percent prime rate, 15 percent long governments. It was ugly. And the economy was really much in a free-fall and people were really worried, 'Is this it? Has the American economy had it? Are we going to be able to control inflation?' I mean there was a lot of very uncertain times. You had to say to yourself, 'I believe it in. I believe in stocks. I believe in companies. I believe they can control this. And this is an anomaly.' Double-digit inflation is rare thing. Doesn't happen very often. And, in fact, one of my shareholders wrote me and said, 'Do you realize that over half the companies in your portfolio are losing money right now?' I looked up, he was right, or she was right. But I was ready. I mean I said, 'These companies are going to do well once the economy comes back. We've got out of every other recession. I don't see why we won't come out of this one.' And it came out and once we came back, the market went north" (Interview with Peter Lynch, PBS). The only way I think systemic risks can be mitigated is to buy great companies that can survive the economic storm and the company should have pricing power allowing the company to raise prices during periods of inflation without losing customers.

Another type of risk is nonsystemic or business-specific risk. The nonsystemic risks can range from financial burdens where the company cannot service their debt obligations, or management makes poor decisions and the company ends up in chapter 11. Other risks may include rules and regulations or political climate that may prevent a business from operating effectively. To prevent this risk, portfolio managers and academics preach diversification. If you have 10 stocks and 5 perform well and the other 5 go sideways, you have done quite well. If you have 20 stocks, then you need to be right on 10 stocks. The more stocks you have, you need to be right more often. Charlie Munger once noted, "The academics have done a terrible disservice to intelligent investors by glorifying the idea of diversification. Because I just think the whole concept is literally almost insane.

SO YOU WANT TO BE A SUPERINVESTOR?

It emphasizes feeling good about not having your investment results depart very much from average investment results." His esteemed Berkshire Hathaway partner Warren Buffett added, "If you can identify six wonderful businesses, that is all the diversification you need. And you will make a lot of money. And I can guarantee that going into a seventh one instead of putting more money into your first one is gotta be a terrible mistake. Very few people have gotten rich on their seventh best idea. But a lot of people have gotten rich with their best idea. So I would say for anyone working with normal capital who really knows the businesses they have gone into, six is plenty, and I probably have half of what I like best. I don't diversify personally" (Diversificationquotes).

In the "Warren Buffett Portfolio," a study was conducted tracking the yearly returns of 3,000 portfolios with 250 stocks, 3,000 portfolios with 100 stocks, 3,000 portfolios with 50 stocks, and 3,000 portfolios with 15 stocks over a ten-year period starting in 1979. The results were as follows:

- 250 stock portfolios—the best return was 16% and worst return was 11.4%
- 100 stock portfolios—the best return was 18.3% and worst return was 10%
- 50 stock portfolios—the best return was 19.1% and worst return was 8.6%
- 15 stock portfolios—the best return was 26.6% and worst return was 4.4%

- Out of 3,000 15 stock portfolios, 808 beat the market
- Out of 3,000 50 stock portfolios, 549 beat the market
- Out of 3,000 100 stock portfolios, 337 beat the market
- Out of 3,000 250 stock portfolios, 63 beat the market

As you can see from the study, once you have more than 15 stocks, adding more stocks does not substantially impact returns. However, it also lowers overall returns and the likelihood of beating the market (Hagstrom 2000).

Volatility

Another term associated with risk is volatility. Academics love to use the term volatility to define risk. This is because volatility is quantifiable and can be used to support the concepts taught in schools. However, volatility and risk are not interchangeable. Short-term volatility is based on people having adverse reactions to changing macroenvironments or the potential damage caused by some news. There is no way to have advance knowledge of the news and to mitigate this so-called risk. It is inevitable your investment will face volatility. The only way to deal with this volatility is by understanding your investment. In the previous sections, I have outlined the key qualities for identifying a great business. There may be a plethora of reasons the market drops, but if the fundamentals that made the business you invested in are not changing with the market, then one should add to the position not sell. On the other hand, volatility may be caused by too much euphoria in the market. If your investment spikes upward on no specific news, you must decide if the stock is unreasonably high and if it is time to take profits.

7.7 You Need to Summarize!

When we look at price first, it is easy to develop a bias toward a certain stock. This is why I like to go through the initial steps of understanding the company, determining if there is a moat, researching management, and evaluating the potential risks to the company. Let's summarize our findings before moving on to price. Write down three reasons—having nothing to do with the stock price—why you want to own the company's stock. Usually a great business is simple to understand: has a large moat, there is a need for the product, the price of the product can be increased to keep up with inflation without the risk of losing customers, and management is aligned with shareholder interests. I have created a guide for you to use. These are sample questions, and you do not need to answer all the questions, but the more of the questions you can answer, the better off you will be.

Understand the business
1. How does the business make money?
2. Can the business have long-term success?
3. Will the business grow in the future?
4. Do customers demand the product(s)?
5. Is there value from the products?
6. Is there a big following?
7. If prices are raised, will customers buy another product?

Moat
8. How is the company positioned in the industry?
9. Does the company have a strong brand?
10. Are there barriers to enter the industry?
11. Are there switching costs?
12. Is there network effects?
13. Is there a price moat?
14. How would a startup with unlimited resources stack up against the company?

Management
15. Is the business so strong that management's main job is to not mess up?
16. Is management aligned with shareholders or their own pockets?
17. Is excess capital employed successfully?
18. Is management truthful or misleading?
19. What is return on equity and return on invested capital?
20. What are the financials telling me?

Risk Management
21. Did I invert the story?
22. Is it systemic or nonsystemic risk?
23. Is their short-term volatility or risk of permanent loss?

7.8 You Need to Find Intrinsic Value!

Price Matters

You have found a wonderful company that has a great story. You made all the inversions to the story and were able to refute every negative point. Now should you buy the stock at any price? No, this is when patience is tested. If you are holding an investment for the long-term, the price you pay makes all the difference. In *The New Buffettology*, Mary Buffett states, "Consider this. In 1991, H&R Block traded between $19 and $38 a share. Ten years later, in 2001, it traded at $80 a share. If you paid $19 for a share back in 1991, and sold it for $80 a share in 2001, then your pretax annual compounding rate of return would be approximately 15.4%. If you paid $38 a share in 1991 and sold it for $80 a share in 2001, then your pretax annual compounding rate of return would be approximately 7.7%. Had you invested $100,000 in H&R Block at $19 a share, in 1991, it would have compounded annually at 15.4% and grown to be worth approximately $418,849 by 2001. If you had invested $100,000 in H&R Block at $38 a share back in 1991, it would have compounded annually at 7.7% and grown to be worth approximately $209,969 by 2001 That's a difference of $208,880! Pay more, earn less. Pay less, earn more" (Buffet and Clark 2002, p.91).

Intrinsic Value

To the common investor and even most professionals, they rely on the stock price to determine if a stock is good or bad. If you have made it this far into the book, you are not a common investor. You have seen there are a lot of factors that determine the value of a stock. You might be wondering, how do I determine if I am buying a stock at a good value? It is nearly impossible to predict the future, but there are some mathematical tools that can help us get an approximation. Being approximately right as opposed to completely wrong is what separates making good or bad investment decisions. I will walk you through how I get an approximate calculation of intrinsic value.

Let's say you are buying a car. You have selected a car that has the color and a sleek look that you want. You make a few assumptions about the car and then determine the value. When you go to the dealer, the price he or she quotes is very different than your value. Suppose you value the car at $20,000. If the car is selling at $30,000, you do some shrewd negotiating to bring the price and value close to being the same, and then a purchase is made. If you budget $20,000 and your dream car is $200,000, there is no point in negotiating, and you simply move on to the next car. Similarly in stocks, we need to make some assumptions on the future growth of stocks to determine a future value, apply a multiple, then use a discount rate to find the value today. All of this sounds like a lot of math, but remember I am "smart lazy." I just plug in numbers from a financial website and use preprogrammed formulas in excel for the computer to do the math.

Gather the Numbers

To make our assumptions on how the business should be valued, we have to rely on previously reported data. You can use any financial website to pull the key financial data. I prefer to use Morningstar as they provide ten years of financial data or less if the company has not been in operation for ten years. Having ten years of operating history allows me to see if the company is consistent or erratic in producing results. To demonstrate the importance of consistency, let's look at two hypothetical companies. The first company has a ten-year earning history with numbers of 1, 2, 6, -5, -9, 3, 1, -6, 2, -9. There is no visible trend, and there is no way to come up with a reasonable estimate of the future earnings. Our second company has ten year earning numbers of 9, 9, 8, 10, 10, 10, 9, 10, 12. We can estimate the future earnings will be between 9 and 10, but it may have outliers of 8 or 12, which are still great numbers.

To begin, gather all the numbers for gross margin (margin after direct costs are taken out), then collect the operating margin numbers (margin after business expenses are taken out). Instead of just taking net margin, I take the numbers for selling, general, and administration as I want this expense to be low and I want the research and development expense to be high as this shows that the company is willing to forgo immediate profits and invest in long-term growth. I also look to see if the company has sufficient liquidity in both the short-term and long-term. The current ratio compares the short-term (current) assets to short-term (current) liabilities. If the company was in a dire situation, it can convert the current assets to cash to pay off all the current liabilities. I like this ratio to be over 1.5. The other ratio is the debt-to-equity ratio, which shows the long-term solvency of a company. Some debt if used effectively can help a business, but too much debt can bankrupt a company. The debt-to-equity ratio compares a company's long-term liabilities to its equity. If this ratio is close to 1, it is a sign the company is using too much leverage for operations and may go bankrupt. Last but not least, I also take the important ROIC and ROE numbers. I have taken Nvidia (NVDA) as an example.

nvda											avg
goss margin	39.8	51.4	52	54.9	55.5	56.1	58.8	59.9	61.2	62	55.16
operating margin	7.2	16.2	15.1	12	16.2	17.5	28	33	32.5	26.1	20.38
sga	11.81	10.15	10.07	10.55	10.27	12.02	9.59	8.39	8.46	10.01	10.132
rd percent	23.96	25.08	26.8	32.34	29.04	26.57	21.17	18.5	20.28	25.91	24.965
current ratio	3.42	4.2	4.89	5.94	6.38	2.48	4.69	8.03	7.94	7.67	5.564
debt to equity	0.01	0.01	—	0.31	0.32	—	0.35	0.27	0.21	0.21	0.21125
roic	8.08	15.38	12.17	8.13	11.09	9.34	22.94	33.68	39.3	20.39	18.05
roe	8.66	15.86	12.54	9.48	14.21	13.82	32.57	46.05	49.26	25.95	22.84

Note: In the final column, I used the =Average (ten numbers) function in excel.

Growth Rates

If you watch any financial news program, eventually you will hear the term *EPS*, or earnings per share. Most analysts come to a consensus of what this number should be. If the company does not

SO YOU WANT TO BE A SUPERINVESTOR?

report earnings that are higher than the consensus, the stock price will fall. The media has led investors to believe earnings beats are the best way to value a stock. By now we know that just blindly listening to the crowd on investment advice can be very dangerous to the investor. Instead, we must ask ourselves why this is a good investment and how fast the investment will grow. The three growth rates I like to use are earnings growth, book value growth, and free cash flow growth.

Book value is equity per share. As you may recall, equity is on the balance sheet and represents the amount of money that would be returned to the company's shareholders if all of the assets were liquidated to pay off debts and the excess money was returned to shareholders. I want to see that equity in the company is growing year over year as I can infer that my investment will also grow in the future.

Free cash flow is the amount of cash the business generates after all of the expenses for maintaining the business are accounted for. I view this as the most important growth rate as this shows if the company can consistently generate excess cash. Each growth rate tells a valuable story, making it necessary to use all three growth rates in our intrinsic value calculations.

nvda											avg
goss margin	39.8	51.4	52	54.9	55.5	56.1	58.8	59.9	61.2	62	55.16
operating margin	7.2	16.2	15.1	12	16.2	17.5	28	33	32.5	26.1	20.38
sga	11.81	10.15	10.07	10.55	10.27	12.02	9.59	8.39	8.46	10.01	10.132
rd percent	23.96	25.08	26.8	32.34	29.04	26.57	21.17	18.5	20.28	25.91	24.965
current ratio	3.42	4.2	4.89	5.94	6.38	2.48	4.69	8.03	7.94	7.67	5.564
debt to equity	0.01	0.01	—	0.31	0.32	—	0.35	0.27	0.21	0.21	0.21125
roic	8.08	15.38	12.17	8.13	11.09	9.34	22.94	33.68	39.3	20.39	18.05
roe	8.66	15.86	12.54	9.48	14.21	13.82	32.57	46.05	49.26	25.95	22.84
eps	0.94	0.9	0.74	1.12	1.08	2.57	4.82	6.63	4.52	6.12	23%
book value	6.77	7.66	7.61	7.72	8.3	9.1	10.48	15.64	18.31	24.7	15%
free cash flow	0.98	1.25	0.96	1.07	1.24	1.79	2.12	4.08	5.41	5.9	22%

Note: To obtain the three growth rates in the last column I used a =RATE (number of years between the beginning and end (9 in this example), blank, -[initial number], final number)

Intrinsic Value with a Margin of Safety

Now that we have our three growth rates, let's start off with finding the future value. I use a future value function in excel: =FV(growth rate, total number of years (10 in this case), blank, -[final number])

fv
49.06565597
104.054703
43.36137562

Next, we need to determine what multiples will the market place on earnings, book value, and free cash flow. The ratio for price to earnings is called the P/E ratio. The ratio for price to book value is called the P/BV ratio. The ratio of price to free cash flow is called the P/FCF ratio. Ideally I would want ten-year averages for the ratios, but I can only find five-year averages on Morningstar. For each of the future values, I multiply by the average multiple found to get a sense of how the market will value the earnings, book value, and free cash flow.

multiple
2347.791638
1428.671072
1681.554147

We now have a conservative estimate of how the company should do in the future and how the market will value the company. However, what is an attractive price to pay today for the investment?

SO YOU WANT TO BE A SUPERINVESTOR?

We first need to ask ourselves, what is the minimum rate of return we want on an investment. For me, if I plan on holding an investment for ten years, then I would like a 20% compounded rate of return (this number is subjective and you can choose a lower or higher rate that aligns with your goals.) To find the present value, I use the present value function in excel:

=PV (minimum accepted value of return, total years, blank, -[calculated multiple])

pv
379.181457
230.7383542
271.5803826

Margin of Safety

What if your assumptions are wrong? If we are wrong and choose to buy at the present value, we may be taking on too much risk for our return. Since I am a conservative investor, I put a high margin of safety (MOS) on the present value.

Let's take an elevator with a weight limit of 2,000 lbs. You are a 150-lb man waiting to take the elevator. As you approach the elevator doors, you notice ten larger men are already inside. You estimate that the ten larger men are between 280–320 lbs each. After this quick estimate, you reason the elevator exceeds the weight limit and is probably toward the upper limit of the excess weight. You can get on, and the elevator might stop or it might be fine. It is probably not worth the risk to get in the elevator. What if the ten people weigh around 200 lbs each? The weight limit is reached, but you can take the risk and squeeze into the elevator. Most likely the addition of 150 lbs will not halt the elevator. It may be worth the risk if you are running late. What if all the people are 150 lbs too? The elevator is well below the weight limit, so you determine there is no risk for you to also get in the elevator.

In our elevator example, the third scenario was ideal as it presented the least amount of risk since the weight was substantially under the margin for excess weight. Similarly when we are making an investment, we may be wrong in our assumptions, so we should apply a margin of safety to limit the risk of being wrong. This concept of margin of safety has been taught by Ben Graham and has been crucial to many value-oriented investors over the years. In his book *Margin of Safety*, Seth Klarman states, "A margin of safety is achieved when securities are purchased at prices sufficiently below underlying value to allow for human error, bad luck, or extreme volatility in a complex, unpredictable and rapidly changing world" (Klarman 1991). The margin of safety should be used to lower the risk of your investment.

To find the *Margin of Safety* price, I multiply the calculated present value by .5.

mos
189.590729
115.369177
135.790191

The average of the three MOS prices is our average buy price, and the average of the three PV price is our sell price.

avg buy	avg sell
146.916699	293.833398

SO YOU WANT TO BE A SUPERINVESTOR?

These calculations are an estimate and should be used as a guide, not a definitive rule. If the company you have researched is above the calculated buy price, buy 10–15% of your desired position if it has all the components of a great business, but you should hope the price falls and you can buy more of the stock at a discount. It is better to get 80% of a stock that doubles than to get 0% of a stock that quadruples. However, if the company is trading 100% higher than your buy price, then it is best to look at another investment. On the other hand, you should not automatically sell once you reach the average sell price. Once the sell price is reached, reassess the qualitative factors and if the fundamentals of the business are improving or declining.

CHAPTER 8
You Need to Do the Research!

The hardest thing in investing is knowing where to begin. There are so many stocks to choose from. To make it even more complicated, there is so much industry research on most stocks that it is easy to get intimidated by so much information and give up. Overwhelmed, you decide to abdicate your power to a portfolio manager.

Well, I will demystify the process for you. Doing your own research on stocks and keeping the power to control your financial future does not need to be hard. To help you on this journey, I will show you where I go to find information on potential investments.

First, I start by thinking about what is going on in the world. At the time of writing, there is a global pandemic. We are seeing that shutdowns are causing turmoil in the markets. Inflation is on the rise again. This has caused shockwaves throughout the market. My feeling is that industries that lead us on the way down will lead us on the way up. There are many industries that should benefit from a reopening. Out of the industries, I asses which one is the easiest for me to understand and what would I enjoy taking a deep dive into.

I also want to look at the other side of the spectrum. As everything reopens and there is extra demand for supplies, this should cause inflation to rise in America. This will affect most of the market, so I want a safer large company that can withstand turmoil. In his 1981 letter to shareholders, Warren Buffet shares insight in investing during inflation and what to look for in stocks. "The first involves companies that, through design or accident, have purchased only businesses that are particularly well adapted to an inflationary environment. Such favored business must have two characteristics: (1) an ability to increase prices rather easily (even when product demand is flat and capacity is not fully utilized) without fear of significant loss of either market share or unit volume, and (2) an ability to accommodate large dollar volume increases in business (often produced more by inflation than by real growth) with only minor additional investment of capital. Managers of ordinary ability, focusing solely on acquisition possibilities meeting these tests, have achieved excellent results in recent decades. However, very few enterprises possess both characteristics, and competition to buy those that do has now become fierce to the point of being self-defeating" (Buffett 1982).

I want to focus on the mega cap companies that can be a safe haven during difficult times, have pricing power, generate lots of cash, have great returns on their investments, and can grow my investment for years to come. Out of the mega cap companies, I have to eliminate the companies that are in an industry that are not in my circle of competence or in an industry that I do not believe will have substantial growth. Once I have identified the industry I want to look at, then I will begin researching multiple investments. By researching at least nine companies, I can find three stalwarts with a unique competitive advantage, three mediocre, and three subpar companies. This exercise also helps me to identify industry jargon and differences in the tone of earning reports and earning call transcripts.

Now we need to research individual stocks. To start, I like to go to Yahoo Finance and trusted investment research websites such as Zacks or Seeking Alpha to get a brief overview of what the company does and the segments of the business. If these summary paragraphs are too complicated and do not make sense to me, I will end my search here. If the summary is intriguing, then I will search for the companies 10-K report.

10K

The annual 10K report can be found on the company's website or through the SEC website. On a 10K, I start by reading the business overview, which is usually in the first section. If a company has a straightforward management that is not trying to hide information, the 10K will contain what the business does, how is the business organized, how the business makes money, if there's an innovative culture, and how management intends to grow the business in the future. This section will highlight if there are any other hidden initiatives that make the company unique and well-positioned to thrive.

Then we come to the section on risks. From reading many 10K reports, I have noticed many middle-of-the-pack companies just use this section as a disclaimer and list all of the macro or general risk factors as possible. Other wonderful companies will address the competition head-on and state what they are doing that is better than the competition. Intently read this section as some of the risks listed are actually strengths. This is where your understanding of the industry comes in. Ask yourself, how likely is this risk to occur? If the risk does occur, is that going to be a fatal blow or create a buying opportunity for the stock? I also like to look at investment research and understand the reasons others would sell the stock. This points out if there are other investment-specific risks that I may have overlooked. I need to be able to refute every concern before putting my hard-earned money in an investment. Ask yourself, what is the probability of the risk actually happening?

In part 2 of a 10K, I look at the selected financial data. After briefly looking at the tables, I try to identify the positive or negative trends. The most important section of a 10K is the management's discussion of the key financial data. It is important to recognize the tone in this section if management is highlighting the company's successes and clearly states how they add value. While reading this section, ask yourself, what is the level of detail in this section? Are all the segments of the business highlighted and does management clearly state how the company makes money? Does management use a negative event to hide behind why they failed to meet expectations, or do they address the issue head-on? Does management skip sections that will shine a negative light on the company? No company is perfect on 100% of their decisions, but we need to evaluate how management reacts to adversity. Now let's move on to the most recent quarterly report.

Note: A company issues three 10Q reports and one 10K report that encompasses a 10Q and full-year report.

10Q and Earnings Call

The 10Q gives us a lot of in-depth detail on the business segments, products, and services the business offers. Usually the first section will highlight what are the company goals and if there is an innovative culture. It is important to trust but verify these statements; we can look at the numbers to actually determine if the R&D efforts are actually useful or just a waste.

Shortly after a 10Q is released, there will be an earnings call to discuss the results of the quarter. On the call, analysts ask pointed questions to management. Pay close attention if management answers all the questions or avoids the questions. Does management actually answer the tough questions, or do they try to divert all the attention to other areas of the business? If management is well prepared, they will have all the facts and tout successes at every opportunity. Read the transcripts carefully as a hidden secret or a key part of the moat may be revealed.

Other Research

If the 10K, 10Q, and financial tables provided enough information that leave me feeling confident about investing, I will do a quick search to read any current news on the company either positive or negative. Finally, I will read some investment research and see if I agree with the listed reasons to buy or sell.

When you go through this exercise, if you have a positive view of the company so far, write up your summary disproving the negative views. If you can explain why the negative view is wrong, you are ready to search a financial website for earnings, book value, and cash flow history to calculate intrinsic value.

PART 4

Buying, Holding, and Selling Stock

CHAPTER 9
You Need to Have Patience in the Market!

Patience

Now that you know how to identify quality stocks and can calculate a good purchase price for a stock, it can be excruciatingly difficult to wait for the price to fall to your buy range. It is natural, especially in a bull market, to start doubting if patience is the best option. This doubt is enhanced by the fact that other investors are making quick money by purchasing hot stocks at any price. Now you are starting to think, *I have money on the sidelines, but stocks are not falling to my margin of safety price and will only go up. I need to buy at any price or miss out.* Do not succumb to the herd. Take a step back, and think about the market sentiment. You will realize that nothing goes on forever, and eventually the market sentiment shifts and stocks go on sale.

Let's say you bought a 50-inch TV for $500 and the TV breaks on October 31st. You can go to the store on November 1 and buy another 50-inch TV for $500. However, you decide to wait until Black Friday and Cyber Monday sales at the end of the month. You may find a 50-inch TV for $300, or there might even be an upgraded 65-inch TV for $500 that you can buy instead. You do not know the exact deal on Black Friday, but based on the past, you know this sale will occur, and it is better to wait patiently to capitalize on a deal. The same applies to the stock market. Deals come by in the stock market very infrequently, but when those deals come, it is best to be ready to capitalize on the opportunity. In the next section, let's examine the importance of waiting for deals in the stock market.

Wait for the Fat Pitch

If you watch any financial program, it is inevitable that you will see an active trader that makes buy or sell decisions daily. The investment community feels the need to act all the time. This is because money managers fear that inaction or missing opportunities in a bull market will cause clients to withdraw their funds and hire a more active money manager. If we are in a bear market, the money manager fears if they take too many losses, clients will take their money out and hand it over to a manager that is promising safety in investments. Individuals can wait for ideal conditions before acting without the fear of losing clients. Not having to serve clients and being able to stick with your investment decisions is the key advantage individuals can have over large money managers. In a 1974 interview in *Forbes* magazine, Warren Buffett stated, "I call investing the greatest business in the world…because you never have to swing. You stand at the plate, the pitcher throws you General Motors at 47, US Steel at 39, and nobody calls a strike on you. There's no penalty except opportunity lost. All day you wait for the pitch you like; then when the fielders are asleep, you step up and hit it" (Forbes 2008).

Again Buffett brought in a baseball analogy in his 1997 letter, "We try to exert a Ted Williams kind of discipline. In his book The Science of Hitting, Ted explains that he carved the strike zone into 77 cells, each the size of a baseball. Swinging only at balls in his 'best' cell, he knew, would allow him to bat .400; reaching for balls in his 'worst' spot, the low outside corner of the strike zone, would reduce him to .230. In other words, waiting for the fat pitch would mean a trip to the Hall of Fame; swinging indiscriminately would mean a ticket to the minors. If they are in the strike zone at all, the business 'pitches' we now see are just catching the lower outside corner. If we swing, we will be locked into low returns. But if we let all of today's balls go by, there can be no assurance that the next ones we see will be more to our liking. Perhaps the attractive prices of the past were the aberrations, not the full prices of today. Unlike Ted, we can't be called out if we resist three pitches that are barely in the strike zone; nevertheless, just standing there, day after day, with my bat on my shoulder is not my idea of fun" (Buffett 1998). His partner in investing Charlie Munger added, "The big money is not in the buying and selling…but in the waiting" (Charlie Munger Quote).

Overnight Rewards

From reading this book, you have devised a well-thought-out plan on how to invest, but at times you see other traders throw a dart at the board only to get lucky and find a stock that goes up 100% in a week. Should you abandon your philosophy and try to speed up the process of investing? No. These "meme" stocks may go up 100% in a week, but eventually the market will turn sour, and the same meme stocks will lose all of their value overnight. This drastic shift can financially ruin any person that had invested in the stock. Also with most of the meme stocks, one might hold the stock for a month or two before selling, which does not allow for compounding. Not only should investors be patient with buying stocks, but they should also be patient holding stocks and allow compounding to work magic over time.

When Berkshire Hathaway was nowhere near being the powerhouse it is today, there was a third partner at the helm, Rick Guerin. Guerin saw others making large amounts of money by speculating and using leverage. He thought that Berkshire Hathaway was moving very slowly and there were better ways to make money quickly elsewhere. In his own fund, Rick Guerin decided to use large amounts of leverage to purchase very risky speculative investments. This strategy did very well initially when the market was going up. Unfortunately the market does not go up in a straight line, and reversed course. Everyone began losing money in the bear market of the '70s. The use of excessive leverage can amplify your profits in a bull market but also worsens losses in a bear market. Guerin was a victim of the change in direction of the market. During a lunch with Warren Buffet in 2007, investor Monish Pabrai recounts his discussion about Rick Guerin.

"Then Rick Guerin pretty much disappeared off the map. I've met Rick recently, but he disappeared off the map, so I asked Warren, are you in touch with Rick, and what happened to Rick? And Warren said, yes, he's very much in touch with him. And he said, Charlie and I always knew that we would become incredibly wealthy. And he said, we were not in a hurry to get wealthy; we knew it would happen. He said, Rick was just as smart as us, but he was in a hurry. And so actually what happened—some of this is public—was that in the '73, '74 downturn, Rick was levered with margin loans. And the stock market went down almost 70% in those two years, and so he got margin calls out the yin-yang, and he sold his Berkshire [Hathaway] (NYSE:BRK.A) (NYSE:BRK.B) stock to Warren. Warren actually said, I bought Rick's Berkshire stock at under $40 apiece, and so Rick was forced to sell shares at…$40 apiece because he was levered" (Hargreaves 2020).

Guerin was eventually able to recover the losses for investors in his fund but proceeded to close his partnership by 1983. The reason is uncertain, but it is thought to be due to the severe losses that Rick Guerin faced. He wanted to recoup the losses for his investors and never wanted to deal with that kind of stress again. The key takeaway should be that by using margin, Guerin was forced to sell Berkshire stock in the '70s at $40, as opposed to holding the stock, which has appreciated to about $470,000 fifty years later. Sometimes slow and steady wins the race.

CHAPTER 10
You Need to Stay with Your Investing Journey!

Periodicity

Even if we had a crystal ball that told us all the major news events, it is still difficult to predict how groups of other investors will react in the stock market. We can't predict when there will be an event or how people will react, but we can predict that most of the reactions to these events can lead to periods of optimism (bull markets) or periods of pessimism (bear markets).

Bull and Bear Markets

Stage 1: Transition from a Bear to Bull Market

When there is pain in the economy, the government will undoubtedly step in to stop the bleeding. The government will usually begin by bailing out the large and vital companies. Then to stabilize the falling economy, the Fed drops interest rates. Companies are able to refinance debt. It is easy for individuals to take out a loan, and there is a rise in earnings making stocks more attractive. A few investors recognize the shift and start buying stocks.

Stage 2: The Start of a Bull Market

More investors realize improvement is actually taking place and start pouring money into the stock market. Many momentum stocks start to see 20–30% gains. Seeing the spectacular results, many prudent investors get swept up in this craze and start moving money out of safer investments and into riskier momentum names. There are a few momentum fund managers that hit home runs. Many new investors want to join the success and start borrowing money to buy the momentum plays.

Stage 3: Random Events Causing Market Corrections and Panics

Right when the bull market is in full swing and investors are on top of the world, there is some geopolitical or economic event that causes the market to pull back. During stock market corrections and panics, stock prices drop for reasons that have nothing to do with the underlying business fundamentals. Since there is no business problem to overcome, the problem is short-lived. This is a perfect buying opportunity for wonderful companies on sale. During the stock market panic of 1987, investors began fleeing the market. The contrarian, Warren Buffett, identified a great business in Coca-Cola that was undervalued due to a correction, not a real business problem. Buffett started buying the undervalued stock and was handsomely rewarded for taking this contrarian view as the market rebounded.

Stage 4: Top of the Bubble

As the market rebounds after a short pullback, many investors conclude that good times will go on forever and put everything they can into the stock market. Stocks begin to trade at P/Es of fifty or higher. The investment community announces that earnings no longer matter and valuations are based on total sales and revenues. Stocks that don't have earnings but have revenues see their share prices soar. In the late 1990s, investment banks would initially price public offerings on the basis of net earnings but suddenly started switching over to total sales and revenues. The banks would fund a start-up company that would generate revenues and take it public. The stock market would value the new public stock at twenty times total sales, making the venture capitalists instantly rich. The pinnacle of this insanity was seen when Jim Clark, one of the founders of Netscape, sold his interest in the company for a billion dollars. Netscape had never made a dime. We also see momentum mutual funds post annual returns of 70% or better. Value-oriented fund managers are forced to capitulate and join the momentum game as all of their clients start pulling their money to invest in momentum funds. This craze can go on for many months or years. This is when the bubble is about to pop and holding cash is a great idea. Once there are no more buyers left, the market begins to decline.

Stage 5: The Bubble Pops and Start of a Bear Market

During this stage, many insiders begin to cash out their positions knowing their company stock is massively overvalued. There are reports of corporate fraud, and there is financial distress. This impacts everyone but is severely damaging to anyone using leverage in the market. During the early bull market phases, everything was going great, so investors only saw how leverage amplified the returns. Now that the market is beginning to tumble, we see the downside of leverage as losses are piling up and banks are making margin calls to recoup the borrowed money and interest owed. If the investors cannot pay the bank back or meet the margin requirements, the broker will liquidate the entire portfolio. The investors who suffered a critical blow from using leverage swear off investing forever. Stocks are now in freefall and sink further. Other investors realize things are deteriorating and sell too. A stock price should only drop to its intrinsic value, but the market is so oversold that wonderful companies are now selling far below intrinsic value. The downturn keeps going on until the government intervenes and a few investors start buying stocks again as they realize the bad times will not last forever. The bear and bull market cycle is about to repeat. The events and stages are the same, but the catalysts that trigger events and the duration is different (Buffett and Clark 2002, pp. 30–35).

Cycles

In the 1970s, there was so much euphoria in the market that many investors would buy anything selling in the stock market regardless of price. Eventually the market did correct and stock prices dropped, leaving people stunned and depressed. The panic caused an emotional reaction, and investors dumped their entire portfolio in a haste. A stock purchased at $150 per share was sold a few weeks later for $90 per share. Nothing changed in the story for many stocks, but herd mentality took over, and many investors sold because that was the popular notion at the time. By the mid-1980s, the stock market had rebounded to the former levels before the panic. This new boom was just the precursor for the next financial panic. The stock market goes through various stages of the cycle at different times. Let's explore some of the causes of the cycle stages.

Economic Cycle

The Fed has a mandate to promote a stable price environment while keeping inflation under control. When the economy slows, the Fed will have an easy money policy and buys securities. With the Fed pumping money into the banking system, the banks are eager to loan money to customers. Since the banks have to compete among themselves to attract new customers, banks lower interest rates, making it easier for consumers to take out a loan. Credit lenders thrive and make it easier for consumers to borrow money by lowering demanded returns (e.g., cutting interest rates), lowering credit standards, providing more capital for a given transaction, and easing covenants. Companies turn to the credit markets to finance growth and refinance maturing debt. With many people and companies being able to access the easy money, there is more spending and the economy expands. From a stock market perspective, we see two factors that raise stock prices. First, as there is more spending and buying of goods or services from a company, earnings and the stock price tend to rise. Second, there is no alternative to where investors can put money as bonds, and other debt instruments pay very low interest rates.

With the expanding economy and the rising demand for goods, there is an excess of money chasing a few goods. This causes prices of goods to rise, causing moderate to high inflation. To combat inflation, the Fed starts tightening the money supply. The Fed now sells securities back to banks. By taking money out of the banking system, the banks are more selective with their lending to customers. Banks now offer loans with higher rates. Only the most credit worthy borrowers are able to borrow from the bank as interest rates, credit restrictions and covenant requirements are high. Companies become starved for capital too. Borrowers are unable to roll over their debts, leading to defaults and bankruptcies. Since there is less spending, the economy starts to shrink. In the stock market, consumers spend less on goods and services from a company, causing that company to struggle to beat earnings. Also as rates rise, newly issued bonds with higher rates are more attractive. Stocks that were previously returning 8% now have to return 10% to be attractive to investors compared to less risky bonds. This causes stock valuations to come down to more reasonable levels.

"From time to time, providers of capital simply turn the spigot on or off—as in so many things, to excess. There are times when anyone can get any amount of capital for any purpose, and times when even the most deserving borrowers can't access reasonable amounts for worthwhile projects. The behavior of the capital markets is a great indicator of where we stand in terms of psychology and a great contributor to the supply of investment bargains" (Marks 2004, p. 10).

It is nearly impossible to predict when or if a trigger event will occur in the economy that impacts the market. Instead of guessing when the events will occur and timing the markets perfectly, a better use of time is to determine where we are in the respective market or economic cycle and where are we headed. Ask yourself two questions to help you asses where we are in the cycle:

1. What is the investor sentiment in the market?
2. How easy is it to borrow for a loan?

Fortunately there are many examples where history has repeated similar boom and bust cycles to give us a better understanding (Marks 2018, pp. 112–121).

History Rhymes

1. South Sea Bubble

In 1711, the British Parliament formed the South Sea Company, which was supposed to manage the national debt. In 1713, the South Sea Company was given a trade monopoly in the region. Then in 1720, the South Sea Company introduced a plan to take over the national debt. The company would pay off the debt with the increased sales from trade profits, and their rising stock sales would be used to swap out the debt. Everyone in London thought this deal was too good to pass on and rushed out to buy the stock. There was so much demand that the price of the company stock tripled overnight. However, the trade profits were not adequate to cover the debt, and in turn, the South Sea Company was just trading the stock proceeds against itself. This viscous cycle was the beginning of a bubble. Eventually the bubble burst, and the stock lost 80% of its value from the peak.

In his book *The Intelligent Investor*, Benjamin Graham writes how rational minded investors can get swept up into the irrational craze and end up financially ruined.

"Back in the spring of 1720, Sir Isaac Newton owned shares in the South Sea Company, the hottest stock in England. Sensing that the market was getting out of hand, the great physicist muttered that he 'could calculate the motions of the heavenly bodies, but not the madness of the people.' Newton dumped his South Sea shares, pocketing a 100% profit totaling £7,000. But just months later, swept up in the wild enthusiasm of the market, Newton jumped back in at a much higher price—and lost £20,000 (or more than $3 million in [2002–2003s] money. For the rest of his life, he forbade anyone to speak the words 'South Sea' in his presence" (Graham 2003, p. 13)

2. Panic of 1873

Very similar to the South Sea bubble, a major crisis began to form after the expansion of railroads during the Civil War. Investors were so fascinated with railroads that they would buy anything with "rail" in the name regardless of price. If investors did not have money to buy a railroad stock, they would borrow money from the bank. Banks lent huge amounts of money to anyone who wanted to be a railroad tycoon.

At that time, one of the biggest banks Jay Cooke & Company had invested heavily in railroads. The bank had overleveraged itself to build the nation's second transcontinental railroad. When the bank did not have money to fund the project, it declared bankruptcy. Nervous bankers saw that such a big bank failed and immediately ran to their banks to withdraw all of their money. The panic spread to banks in Washington, DC, Pennsylvania, New York, Virginia, and Georgia, as well as to banks in the Midwest, including those in Indiana, Illinois, and Ohio. Many of the banks did not have money available to pay people back, resulting in at least one hundred banks failing nationwide. (Department of Treasury 2022).

Since many investors bought on margin, the pain was amplified. In 1873, an investor only needed to put 10% down for a margin loan. Let's say the investor wanted to buy $10,000 worth of stocks, the investor would pay $1,000, and the bank would offer a loan of $9,000. The margin investor hopes that the investment gains in value by the time they sell. The investor would be able to pay off the loan of $9,000 and the interest accrued. The excess cash would be pure profit. However, during the crash, the $10,000 investment was reduced to $5,000, but the bank still demands $9,000 back. The investor needs to pay the $9,000 plus interest regardless of the economic conditions.

Many margin investors could not pay their debts and filed for bankruptcy. Since the banks had also lost money, they began to fail too, and the economic system was on the verge of collapse.

3. Market Crash of 1929

After World War I, the United States emerged as a dominant economy and entered a period of excess. The Fed was lowering rates, which in turn spurred the economy. People were making many big purchases in automobiles and other luxurious items. Auto sales rose from 1.2 million to 3.6 million annually between 1921 and 1923. This prosperity went on for almost a decade, and investors thought this would go on forever. They started speculating and took out margin loans to buy rising stocks. Over the course of 1927, margin loans grew from $3.29 billion to $4.43 billion. Banks were making money hand over fist. Banks could borrow from the Fed at 5% and lend it to the brokerages at 10% to 12%. As the market rose, so did the number of margin loans. Over 500,000 people were trading on margin. Financial innovations like investment trusts were formed and sold to the public. The sole purpose of investment trusts was to buy and sell stocks using leverage, and a few were created to create new trusts. Unfortunately, good times do not last forever, and eventually the market started to break down. On September 5, 1929, Roger Babson remarked, "I repeat what I said at this time last year and the year before, that sooner or later a crash is coming." This started a chain of selling with the worst coming on Black Tuesday of October 29, 1929. The downturn continued until November 13, 1929. By this time, $30 billion dollars of value (out of $80 billion or 38%) had been wiped out from stocks listed on the NYSE since September. This popping of the bubble was just the precursor for the Great Depression (Brooks 1999).

4. Black Monday of 1987

In the years leading up to 1987, there had been a raging bull market since 1982. A new innovation of computer, or "program trading," was becoming popular in the mid-'80s. Brokers were able to place and execute large trades quickly. Many institutions developed software programs that would sell positions if stocks dropped by a certain percentage. Another tactic was to short the index as it fell. This automated trading strategy was used as a hedge of risk and was called portfolio insurance. If a portfolio of stocks declined, trade orders to sell the index would be automatically executed.

Then in 1987, there were growing concerns with rising oil prices, interest rates, inflation, and trade deficits. This led to a lot of downward pressure in the market. On October 19, 1987, the market broke down. As the market fell, automated trading programs sold many positions once they hit their threshold. As the market was rolling downhill, this also triggered portfolio insurance, and the index was sold. This accelerated selling even further. When trading closed for the day, both the S&P 500 and Dow Jones indices shed 20% of their value (Bermhardt and Eckblad).

This flash crash could not be anticipated, and many historians differ on what actually caused the panic. The key takeaway here is that there are always sudden moves in the market. It is impossible to time the market, and trying to time the markets can be futile and detrimental to a portfolio in the long run. Sometimes, there is no way to avoid a market downturn, and one is better off focusing on what he or she can control.

5. Dot-Com Bubble

During the early 1990s, the web browser made it much easier for the public to access the Internet. Everyone was feeling euphoric. The Internet was going to change the world. Everyone wanted to be a part of this revolution. If you did not have a brokerage account, you had to get one and buy as many tech stocks as possible. Investment banks and venture capital firms would lend generously to help new tech startups list their IPO (initial public offering of stock) in the market. Droves of investors would buy these IPOs that had no earnings and traded on multiples of revenues. Buying internet stocks was the easiest way to become an overnight millionaire. There was only greed in the market. Investors had a new mantra: "Get on board before you miss out. No price is too excessive as the market is always efficient." Failing to buy made investors look like laggards. Even Warren Buffett who avoided investing in tech was ridiculed for not joining the craze.

Just like all cycles, nothing goes on forever. Once investors started expecting real growth and earnings from all the new companies, the party was over. During the decline, the Nasdaq that was filled with the new tech companies had a major decline and did not fully rebound until a decade later. Many corporate scandals were uncovered for companies like Enron "cooking the books" to make the results seem better than they actually were. By 2002, the greed in the market dissipated and no one wanted to be in the market. Prudent investors like Buffett, who avoided the top tech stocks during the craze, were able to survive the crash, come out unscathed, and capitalize on buying wonderful companies that were severely undervalued in 2002 (TheStreet Staff 2022).

6. Financial Crises of 2008

In the early 2000s, the government wanted to increase homeownership and decided to relax many rules for homebuyers. The Fed lowered rates to make it easier to borrow to buy a house. The banks created financial products like CMOs (collateralized mortgage obligations) and CDOs (collateralized debt obligations) to package mortgage and debt loans that contained subprime debt. These novel financial weapons of mass destruction were then sold to other investors who would take on the risk. Other protective rules were relaxed that allowed institutions and traders to partake in this risky behavior. Risk was eliminated because people thought the Fed would always inject stimulus money into the economy. Since this was a sure thing, many investors used margin to purchase CMO and CDO securities.

Eventually the housing markets became saturated, and the Fed started raising rates. With the actions of the Fed and the saturation in the market, home prices began to fall. Since there were no more buyers, homeowners could not sell their declining home asset. To make matters worse, many of the borrowers had adjustable-rate mortgages and could not pay the banks back the loans with the rising interest on the loan. Many borrowers defaulted on their debts. With the increasing defaults, investors that held MBS (mortgage-backed securities) with subprime mortgages lost money. By 2007, there was a steep decline in the value of all MBS. This had caused major losses at many banks, hedge funds, and mortgage lenders. Many institutions failed; while a few survived by appealing to the government for loans, others had to seek mergers with healthier companies. Even firms that were not immediately threatened sustained losses in the billions of dollars as the MBS in which they had invested so heavily were now downgraded by credit-rating agencies. The MBS eventually were deemed "toxic" (essentially worthless) assets. This led to the reluctance for banks lending to borrowers or other banks. The illiquidity created a credit freeze in the financial system and a corresponding tumble in the stock market (Booth and Duca 2007).

Key Takeaways

No two bubbles are exactly the same, but there is usually a common thread. Before any stock market bubble: there tends to be a long period of economic expansion. The government has an easy monetary policy, making it easier to borrow money. New innovations are formed that will "revolutionize" life as we know it. Financial institutions want to capitalize on the hype and create financial products to be sold to the public. Investors fear they will miss out and buy the newly created securities at any price. New trading accounts are opened, and there are record trading volumes among the short-term traders. Short-term traders think it is easy to become a millionaire overnight and continue buying stocks. If an investor is not buying into the hype, they will be ridiculed. This self-feeding frenzy goes on until a saturation point is reached. There also may be a failure of the new innovation to deliver spectacular results, or an unforeseen geopolitical or economic event occurs. The market hates uncertainty, and the optimism now becomes panic. This downtrend will go on until there is some sort of government intervention or policy change. If this does not solve the issue, the country can slide further into recession, or worse, depression, and stock prices will fall further.

We cannot pinpoint exactly when events will occur in the cycle, but it is important to figure out where we are heading. In his book *Mastering the Market Cycle*, Howard Marks states, "The tendency of people to go to excess will never end. And thus, since those excesses eventually have to correct, neither will the occurrence of cycles. Economies and markets have never moved in a straight line in the past, and neither will they do so in the future. And that means investors with the ability to understand cycles will find opportunities for profit" (Marks 2018, p. 227). As long as you can identify patterns and seize the opportunities the market offers, those may be the most important two factors in your investing journey. In addition, not all events that are most likely to occur will happen, so it is always important to be prepared for the unknown by not overextending your portfolio in either direction during good or bad times.

10.2 Positioning

As we have seen throughout history, the most dangerous times in investing comes when people believe risk is nonexistent, they are using unmanageable leverage, and fear missing out on opportunities. Investors should always be cognizant of how others are acting in the market and maintain an adequate amount of defensiveness or aggressiveness depending on the situation. It all comes down to finding the balance in a portfolio and proper allocation.

Allocation

Most portfolio managers say you should shift your asset allocation as you age. What does age have to do with investing? The cycles occur at random. Should a fifty-year-old investor be allocated in 50% bonds and 50% stocks during one of the greatest bull markets to date? Should a thirty-year-old be fully invested during high periods of inflation? A prudent investor should keep an eye on the cycle to asses when sentiment is irrational and when prices have significantly diverged from value. This is the time to sell into optimism to generate cash or to move into safer investments to protect yourself when the bubble pops. Once the bubble pops and everything is being oversold, you will have a fortress of cash to buy wonderful undervalued stocks. Age should not be the dominant factor in making an investing decision.

In his book the *Warren Buffett Portfolio*, Robert Hagstrom outlines the criteria Buffett uses in determining how much money to allocate to a certain stock.

1. The certainty with which the long-term economic characteristics of the business can be evaluated
2. The certainty with which management can be evaluated, both as to its ability to realize the full potential of the business and to wisely employ its cash flows
3. The certainty with which management can be counted on to channel the rewards from the business to the shareholders rather than to itself
4. The purchase price of the business

When one is certain the odds are in your favor, bet heavily. Before starting a new position, take a look at your existing portfolio, and ask yourself how attractive this new investment is compared to my best current investment. If this new investment is not as good as your best investment, you should add to your best investment. Do not add a new investment for the sake of adding a new investment just to be diversified (Hagstrom 2000).

One Time Events: Warren Buffett Bets Heavily on American Express

In the early 1960s, American Express had recently created a new division that specialized in field warehousing. The newly created division made loans to businesses, notably Allied Crude Vegetable

Oil and Refining Company, using inventories as collateral. American Express would send inspectors to check the inventories for the company and then wrote receipts that Anthony De Angelis of Allied Crude Vegetable Oil and Refining Company would take to a bank or a broker to receive cash. Seeing this was an easy way to make money, De Angelis would fill the tanks with seawater and a small amount of oil that would float to the top. Some of the tanks were connected with pipes so oil could be sent from tank to tank during inspections. The fooled inspectors issued many receipts for 1.8 billion pounds of oil, against the supposed inventory that was actually 110 million pounds. The oil containers that Allied was using turned out to be filled mostly with seawater. The small volume of salad oil naturally floated on top of the water and the fraud had thus gone undetected when the containers had been inspected. In 1963, American Express received an anonymous tip they were being conned by Allied Crude. When this fraud was discovered, the share price of American Express fell by more than 50%.

    Even prior to the scandal, American Express was on Warren Buffett's radar as he was impressed with the core business in travelers checks and the brand. Viewing this as a one-time event that would not impact the long-term prospects of the company, Buffett knew he had to seize the opportunity when the stock price dropped rapidly and bet big. In the book *The Snowball: Warren Buffett and the Business of Life*, author Alice Schroeder writes of the event, quoting Buffett himself, "So every trust department in the United States panicked, recalls Buffett. I remember the Continental Bank held over 5 percent of the company, and all of a sudden not only do they see that the trust accounts were going to have stock worth zero, but they could get assessed. The stock just poured out, of course, and the market got slightly inefficient for a short period of time." By thinking in terms of allocation and the probability of outcomes, Buffett put 40% of his partnership's assets in American Express shares. Within three years, the shares rose from $35 to $70 due to the core business fundamental growth. The quick double from American Express resulted in a return twice that of the S&P 500 over the same period (Wathen 2017).

CHAPTER 11
You Should Not Be Quick to Sell!

As we saw in the previous chapter, an investor should not be spooked into selling a stock due to the macro environment. The cardinal sin in investing is selling too early and failing to participate in the cyclical rebound. From 1900 to 2017, the S&P 500 had sixteen bear markets. During these times when the markets slump by more than 20%, it is easy to panic and sell or to mimic institutions that are forced to sell due to downgrades, index additions/removals, bankruptcies, margin calls, liquidations, or spinoffs. These institutional investors cannot hold on to stocks during major declines, since clients will withdraw their money. This is an advantage for us smaller investors as we do not need to serve any clients and can afford to make unemotional decisions.

On the other hand, during good times a stock may go up 50%, and people say sell it and take profits. What if the stock goes up another 100 to 200% after the initial rise? You are either mad at yourself for taking the small profits when you could have had a fairly large return. If you were lucky enough to reinvest after the 50% gain, all that you have done is generate a second tax bill. So when is it okay to sell?

When to Sell

When we identified how to buy stocks in chapter 7, we summarized the story of the stock and we listed reasons to buy. Before selling, reexamine the original thesis and fundamentals of the company. Also asses where the company sits relative to its growth cycle. If there are fundamental changes to the story, the price has appreciated significantly to the point that there is no value, or there are other reinvestment opportunities, those should be the three primary reasons to sell. All macro factors, taxation, pruning, or other reasons are secondary. Some questions to ask before selling are the following:

1. Who's wrong and making a mistake here, the buyer or the seller?
2. Is there a good (business) reason for the price drop?
3. Is there hidden value?
4. Is the general industry in decline?
5. What changed recently?

If the story hasn't changed, there is no reason to sell.

PART 5

Closing Remarks

CHAPTER 12
You Can Learn a Lot from Key Mistakes

From numerous examples in history, keen observations, the wisdom of others, and from my experiences, the most important factors in investing are selecting an exceptional durable company's stock, holding for the long-term, managing emotions, and being able to seize on opportunities. Investing does have some downside risk. No investor has a 100% success rate. You will also have your fair share of mistakes during your investing journey. The key is to learn from your mistakes and become a better investor after each mistake. Here are some mistakes I and other investors have made in the past. I hope you can learn from these mistakes and save yourself from making the same mistakes in the future.

1. Overconfidence

There is a common mistake investors make after they selected a few winners. Investors become overconfident with their selections and think they are always going to hit home runs. No investor in the world is right 100% of the time. If you are right more times than you are wrong, you will do fine. If you allocate more to your winners than losers, you can generate superior results. Once you have made a selection, only put in enough money in the stock that you are comfortable with losing, as you can lose 100% of your money if you are wrong about this stock. Even though you have had major successes in the past, do not skip steps and forget to research stocks before making a purchase. Even if you are not adding to the position, do not forget to monitor the stock. Pay attention to the quarterly reports to stay up to date and to determine if holding the position is the best course of action.

2. *Interrupting Compounding*

Compounding takes time to see spectacular results. Therefore, one should only invest money that is not needed right away. Now there may be an unknown expense that forces a person to take money out of investments, but for the most part, a person should only invest money he or she does not need on a daily basis. Before investing, a person should know their monthly living expenses and how much money can be saved. Since the saved money will not be needed tomorrow, that money should be allocated into investments that can compound over time.

3. *Managing Emotions*

During times of greed and immense speculation, it is hard to resist buying hot stocks. On a few instances, you may get lucky and see your speculative investment go up 400% in a week, as there is even more hype around the stock you pile in more money. Just when you are feeling on top of the world, the market turns unexpectedly, and now the price has fallen to half of the initial purchase price. There is no more hype around the stock. Since this speculative stock has fallen so far, you think, *How low can it go?* You compound the error and add more money to the stock that never rebounds.

Instead of speculating on a company with no earnings, it is much easier to asses a wonderful company with earnings, cash flow, and book value growth to determine the intrinsic value. If you have found a wonderful company and determined the true intrinsic value, you can make decisions to buy when the stock is undervalued and sell when it is vastly overvalued. By understanding intrinsic value, you will limit making decisions on emotions but rather let value dictate decisions. In addition to value, understand where we are in the cycle. In a down leg of the market when fear is piling up and there is mass selling that can cause prices to fall well below intrinsic value, don't be overly eager to buy a stock because you think the market has bottomed. Wait until much of the pain has exited the market. In his book *One Up on Wall Street*, Peter Lynch says it is too hard to pick a bottom. Most of the time when investors go bottom fishing, it is the investor that gets hooked. "Trying to catch the bottom on a falling stock is like trying to catch a falling knife. It's normally a good idea to wait until the knife hits the ground and sticks, then vibrates for a while and settles down before you try to grab it" (Lynch and Rothchild 2000).

4. *Not Having Cash*

During good times, I would always say to myself, *Why should I hold cash in my account?* It is not earning any money, and I can make so much more money being fully invested. My overconfidence contributed to my biggest investing mistake yet. During the market crash of 2020, I was looking at a defense and aerospace stock that was trading at $620. When air travel was shut down and there was no demand for new planes, the stock plummeted to a little bit above $200. If I had a large cash position, this would have been a great buying opportunity. Since the company is so vital to the industry, it quickly rebounded, and in 2022, the same stock was trading near $620 again.

I started to look deeper as to why having cash was crucial during good times. My jaw dropped when I found out Berkshire Hathaway, led by the best investor in the world Warren Buffett, has a large cash position (over $140 billion) even during good times. This quote from Buffett stood out to me, "If you want to shoot rare, fast-moving elephants, you should always carry a loaded gun" (Hagstrom 1997).

In this analogy, Buffett is comparing these industry giants to fast moving elephants, and the ammo needed is cash to purchase the stock of these industry giants. It is very rare when the industry giants tumble, and in this case, it happened due to the unforeseen shutdowns in 2020. If an investor had cash on hand and was able to buy during this big opportunity, they were quickly rewarded.

5. *Giving Up Too Quickly*

Recently, I had researched a company, and it had a good story, was well managed, and met all of the checks listed in chapter 7. I began buying the stock at $19 a share. The stock was moving up to $21 and then falling back to $18. The mistake I made was looking at other companies in the industry that I bought at the time of this purchase. The other stocks in my portfolio in the same industry had gained close to 50% in a few months. I became frustrated and told myself once the stock gets to $21 again, I will sell. Once I sold the stock after three months, my original thesis was proven true. The stock is now trading near $34 a share. This mistake was due to my lack of patience, letting my emotions get in the way, and being overconfident I thought I can do this all over again with ease.

CHAPTER 13
You Can Put It All Together

I am a big UFC fan. After watching numerous fights and seeing that the patient fighter usually wins, I came up with this anecdote that has helped me think of the market and responses an investor should take.

We have two fighters, one fighter is a rational investor like you (A), and the other fighter is the market (B). When the fight begins, both fighters (A) and (B) begin the "feel out" process. Both fighters land a few strikes but usually nothing substantial that definitively wins the round. This is equivalent to the tug-of-war between an investor and the normal day-to-day gyrations of the market. Day after day, the investor is going through the motions of the market cycle, and there is no need for drastic action. Some days the market is up, and other days it falls slightly. There is no significant price action.

As the fight progresses, both fighters trade jabs, and eventually fighter (A) lands a significant strike. Fighter (A) has kept a steady pace and has gotten off a few good hits without expending too much energy. It is still early, and fighter (B) can quickly recover. Then in a split second, fighter (B) makes a mistake, and fighter (A) quickly capitalizes. This is similar to an investor maintaining and balancing the portfolio during normal times, and then out of nowhere, a quick opportunity strikes, and the investor can deploy some cash for a new or existing position in the portfolio. However, this was just a minor event, and the market goes back to acting normally.

Close to the end of the fight, fighter (B) realizes he is behind on the scorecard and cannot let the fight go to decision. The only option fighter (B) has is to knock out the opponent. Fighter (B) starts throwing wild punches, hoping a devasting blow lands. However, the alert fighter (A) can easily evade the punches. This is similar to when the market is getting irrational and is drastically overbought or oversold. The rational investor just has to avoid getting caught up in this erratic behavior.

Inevitably, fighter (B) will make a mistake with his wild punches, and his hands will be out of position to protect his face. Fighter (A) capitalizes on this mistake and lands a huge strike to wobble his opponent. Then fighter (A) charges the opponent and unleashes a barrage of punches to win the fight. During periods of an irrational market, the market will overshoot in the current direction and misprices a security. The patient investor recognizes this mistake and deploys large amounts of cash to eventually "blitz" the market. The opportunistic investor has taken advantage of the market mispricing securities and has acquired amazing companies at bargain prices that will "beat" the market.

Most investors think to be successful in investing, they need to possess superior skill. While skill is needed (to identify wonderful companies), there is no substitute for having patience and being aggressive at the right time. In his book *Mastering the Market Cycle: Getting the Odds on Your Side*, Howard Marks states, "There are three ingredients for success—aggressiveness, timing and skill—and if you have enough aggressiveness at the right time, you don't need that much skill" (Marks 2018, p. 196).

Before wrapping up, I want to remind readers to not be afraid of the market, trust your research ability, be patient waiting for opportunities, and always be in position to take advantage of opportunities when the market starts to rain gold.

APPENDIX 1

Tables

Table 1.1: Annual returns for investments in S&P 500, 3-month T-Bills, US T-Bonds, Baa corporate bonds, and real estate from 1928

Year	S&P 500 (includes dividends)	3-month T-Bill	US T-Bond	Baa Corporate Bond	Real Estate
1928	43.81%	3.08%	0.84%	3.22%	1.49%
1929	-8.30%	3.16%	4.20%	3.02%	-2.06%
1930	-25.12%	4.55%	4.54%	0.54%	-4.30%
1931	-43.84%	2.31%	-2.56%	-15.68%	-8.15%
1932	-8.64%	1.07%	8.79%	23.59%	-10.47%
1933	49.98%	0.96%	1.86%	12.97%	-3.81%
1934	-1.19%	0.28%	7.96%	18.82%	2.91%
1935	46.74%	0.17%	4.47%	13.31%	9.77%
1936	31.94%	0.17%	5.02%	11.38%	3.22%
1937	-35.34%	0.28%	1.38%	-4.42%	2.56%
1938	29.28%	0.07%	4.21%	9.24%	-0.87%
1939	-1.10%	0.05%	4.41%	7.98%	-1.30%
1940	-10.67%	0.04%	5.40%	8.65%	3.31%
1941	-12.77%	0.13%	-2.02%	5.01%	-8.38%
1942	19.17%	0.34%	2.29%	5.18%	3.33%
1943	25.06%	0.38%	2.49%	8.04%	11.45%
1944	19.03%	0.38%	2.58%	6.57%	16.58%
1945	35.82%	0.38%	3.80%	6.80%	11.78%
1946	-8.43%	0.38%	3.13%	2.51%	24.10%
1947	5.20%	0.60%	0.92%	0.26%	21.26%
1948	5.70%	1.05%	1.95%	3.44%	2.06%
1949	18.30%	1.12%	4.66%	5.38%	0.09%
1950	30.81%	1.20%	0.43%	4.24%	3.64%

1951	23.68%	1.52%	-0.30%	-0.19%	6.05%
1952	18.15%	1.72%	2.27%	4.44%	4.41%
1953	-1.21%	1.89%	4.14%	1.62%	11.52%
1954	52.56%	0.94%	3.29%	6.16%	0.92%
1955	32.60%	1.73%	-1.34%	2.04%	0.00%
1956	7.44%	2.63%	-2.26%	-2.35%	0.91%
1957	-10.46%	3.23%	6.80%	-0.72%	2.72%
1958	43.72%	1.77%	-2.10%	6.43%	0.66%
1959	12.06%	3.39%	-2.65%	1.57%	0.11%
1960	0.34%	2.88%	11.64%	6.66%	0.77%
1961	26.64%	2.35%	2.06%	5.10%	0.98%
1962	-8.81%	2.77%	5.69%	6.50%	0.32%
1963	22.61%	3.16%	1.68%	5.46%	2.14%
1964	16.42%	3.55%	3.73%	5.16%	1.26%
1965	12.40%	3.95%	0.72%	3.19%	1.66%
1966	-9.97%	4.86%	2.91%	-3.45%	1.22%
1967	23.80%	4.31%	-1.58%	0.90%	2.32%
1968	10.81%	5.34%	3.27%	4.85%	4.13%
1969	-8.24%	6.67%	-5.01%	-2.03%	6.99%
1970	3.56%	6.39%	16.75%	5.65%	8.22%
1971	14.22%	4.33%	9.79%	14.00%	4.24%
1972	18.76%	4.07%	2.82%	11.41%	2.98%
1973	-14.31%	7.03%	3.66%	4.32%	3.42%
1974	-25.90%	7.83%	1.99%	-4.38%	10.07%
1975	37.00%	5.78%	3.61%	11.05%	6.77%
1976	23.83%	4.97%	15.98%	19.75%	8.18%
1977	-6.98%	5.27%	1.29%	9.95%	14.65%
1978	6.51%	7.19%	-0.78%	3.14%	15.72%
1979	18.52%	10.07%	0.67%	-2.01%	13.74%
1980	31.74%	11.43%	-2.99%	-3.32%	7.40%
1981	-4.70%	14.03%	8.20%	8.46%	5.10%
1982	20.42%	10.61%	32.81%	29.05%	0.56%
1983	22.34%	8.61%	3.20%	16.19%	4.75%
1984	6.15%	9.52%	13.73%	15.62%	4.68%
1985	31.24%	7.48%	25.71%	23.86%	7.47%
1986	18.49%	5.98%	24.28%	21.49%	9.61%
1987	5.81%	5.78%	-4.96%	2.29%	7.88%
1988	16.54%	6.67%	8.22%	15.12%	7.21%
1989	31.48%	8.11%	17.69%	15.79%	4.38%
1990	-3.06%	7.49%	6.24%	6.14%	-0.69%
1991	30.23%	5.38%	15.00%	17.85%	-0.16%
1992	7.49%	3.43%	9.36%	12.17%	0.82%
1993	9.97%	3.00%	14.21%	16.43%	2.16%
1994	1.33%	4.25%	-8.04%	-1.32%	2.51%
1995	37.20%	5.49%	23.48%	20.16%	1.80%
1996	22.68%	5.01%	1.43%	4.79%	2.42%

SO YOU WANT TO BE A SUPERINVESTOR?

1997	33.10%	5.06%	9.94%	11.83%	4.02%
1998	28.34%	4.78%	14.92%	7.95%	6.45%
1999	20.89%	4.64%	-8.25%	0.84%	7.68%
2000	-9.03%	5.82%	16.66%	9.33%	9.28%
2001	-11.85%	3.39%	5.57%	7.82%	6.67%
2002	-21.97%	1.60%	15.12%	12.18%	9.56%
2003	28.36%	1.01%	0.38%	13.53%	9.82%
2004	10.74%	1.37%	4.49%	9.89%	13.64%
2005	4.83%	3.15%	2.87%	4.92%	13.51%
2006	15.61%	4.73%	1.96%	7.05%	1.73%
2007	5.48%	4.35%	10.21%	3.15%	-5.40%
2008	-36.55%	1.37%	20.10%	-5.07%	-12.00%
2009	25.94%	0.15%	-11.12%	23.33%	-3.85%
2010	14.82%	0.14%	8.46%	8.35%	-4.12%
2011	2.10%	0.05%	16.04%	12.58%	-3.88%
2012	15.89%	0.09%	2.97%	10.12%	6.44%
2013	32.15%	0.06%	-9.10%	-1.06%	10.72%
2014	13.52%	0.03%	10.75%	10.38%	4.51%
2015	1.38%	0.05%	1.28%	-0.70%	5.21%
2016	11.77%	0.32%	0.69%	10.37%	5.31%
2017	21.61%	0.93%	2.80%	9.72%	6.21%
2018	-4.23%	1.94%	-0.02%	-2.76%	4.53%
2019	31.21%	1.55%	9.64%	15.33%	3.69%
2020	18.02%	0.09%	11.33%	10.41%	10.35%
2021	28.47%	0.06%	-4.42%	0.93%	16.83%

Table 1.2: Nominal value of $500 invested in the S&P 500, 3-month T-Bills, US T-Bonds, Baa corporate bonds, and real estate from 1928

Year	S&P 500 (includes dividends)	3-month T-Bill	US T-Bond	Baa Corporate Bond	Real Estate
1928	$719.06	$515.40	$504.18	$516.10	$507.46
1929	$659.39	$531.69	$525.37	$531.67	$497.02
1930	$493.73	$555.88	$549.23	$534.54	$475.65
1931	$277.29	$568.72	$535.17	$450.72	$436.88
1932	$253.32	$574.80	$582.22	$557.05	$391.15
1933	$379.94	$580.32	$593.02	$629.28	$376.24
1934	$375.43	$581.94	$640.24	$747.68	$387.18
1935	$550.90	$582.91	$668.88	$847.18	$424.99
1936	$726.88	$583.92	$702.44	$943.63	$438.67
1937	$470.02	$585.53	$712.13	$901.95	$449.91

1938	$607.66	$585.91	$742.13	$985.26	$445.98
1939	$600.99	$586.18	$774.88	$1,063.91	$440.18
1940	$536.85	$586.39	$816.74	$1,155.92	$454.73
1941	$468.28	$587.15	$800.22	$1,213.80	$416.60
1942	$558.07	$589.16	$818.59	$1,276.67	$430.49
1943	$697.93	$591.40	$838.97	$1,379.38	$479.76
1944	$830.75	$593.64	$860.60	$1,469.95	$559.33
1945	$1,128.34	$595.90	$893.34	$1,569.90	$625.20
1946	$1,033.23	$598.16	$921.28	$1,609.27	$775.89
1947	$1,086.95	$601.76	$929.76	$1,613.49	$940.87
1948	$1,148.96	$608.04	$947.90	$1,668.95	$960.24
1949	$1,359.26	$614.82	$992.10	$1,758.69	$961.10
1950	$1,777.98	$622.22	$996.36	$1,833.24	$996.08
1951	$2,198.98	$631.67	$993.42	$1,829.74	$1,056.32
1952	$2,598.12	$642.55	$1,015.95	$1,911.00	$1,102.87
1953	$2,566.73	$654.70	$1,058.05	$1,941.96	$1,229.89
1954	$3,915.89	$660.84	$1,092.86	$2,061.55	$1,241.23
1955	$5,192.36	$672.24	$1,078.25	$2,103.70	$1,241.23
1956	$5,578.65	$689.90	$1,053.93	$2,054.21	$1,252.58
1957	$4,995.27	$712.15	$1,125.57	$2,039.44	$1,286.63
1958	$7,179.20	$724.76	$1,101.94	$2,170.57	$1,295.14
1959	$8,044.76	$749.30	$1,072.78	$2,204.75	$1,296.56
1960	$8,071.83	$770.91	$1,197.64	$2,351.65	$1,306.49
1961	$10,221.98	$789.05	$1,222.32	$2,471.59	$1,319.26
1962	$9,321.28	$810.94	$1,291.92	$2,632.13	$1,323.51
1963	$11,429.00	$836.56	$1,313.68	$2,775.96	$1,351.88
1964	$13,305.12	$866.23	$1,362.65	$2,919.24	$1,368.90
1965	$14,954.85	$900.43	$1,372.45	$3,012.37	$1,391.60
1966	$13,463.71	$944.22	$1,412.36	$2,908.58	$1,408.62
1967	$16,668.47	$984.88	$1,390.03	$2,934.62	$1,441.25
1968	$18,471.15	$1,037.46	$1,435.55	$3,076.81	$1,500.83
1969	$16,948.87	$1,106.62	$1,363.57	$3,014.50	$1,605.80
1970	$17,552.45	$1,177.35	$1,592.03	$3,184.80	$1,737.73
1971	$20,048.60	$1,228.36	$1,747.84	$3,630.72	$1,811.49
1972	$23,808.79	$1,278.39	$1,797.11	$4,044.95	$1,865.40
1973	$20,402.22	$1,368.28	$1,862.86	$4,219.62	$1,929.23
1974	$15,117.68	$1,475.42	$1,899.90	$4,034.77	$2,123.58
1975	$20,710.49	$1,560.62	$1,968.40	$4,480.61	$2,267.42
1976	$25,646.00	$1,638.25	$2,283.04	$5,365.65	$2,452.85
1977	$23,855.99	$1,724.57	$2,312.49	$5,899.79	$2,812.31
1978	$25,408.84	$1,848.54	$2,294.51	$6,084.90	$3,254.50
1979	$30,114.43	$2,034.67	$2,309.89	$5,962.65	$3,701.75
1980	$39,671.32	$2,267.32	$2,240.83	$5,764.94	$3,975.57
1981	$37,805.82	$2,585.31	$2,424.57	$6,252.80	$4,178.12
1982	$45,525.41	$2,859.72	$3,220.18	$8,069.39	$4,201.67
1983	$55,694.49	$3,105.97	$3,323.23	$9,376.17	$4,401.23

SO YOU WANT TO BE A SUPERINVESTOR?

1984	$59,117.55	$3,401.73	$3,779.62	$10,840.65	$4,607.13
1985	$77,583.01	$3,656.15	$4,751.45	$13,427.51	$4,951.34
1986	$91,931.66	$3,874.73	$5,905.31	$16,312.48	$5,427.28
1987	$97,275.39	$4,098.50	$5,612.37	$16,686.02	$5,854.75
1988	$113,362.01	$4,371.76	$6,073.91	$19,208.12	$6,276.90
1989	$149,042.91	$4,726.39	$7,148.61	$22,241.02	$6,551.91
1990	$144,475.57	$5,080.55	$7,594.35	$23,606.63	$6,506.61
1991	$188,157.53	$5,353.63	$8,733.85	$27,821.23	$6,496.33
1992	$202,257.54	$5,537.35	$9,551.48	$31,207.71	$6,549.43
1993	$222,416.65	$5,703.33	$10,908.84	$36,335.61	$6,690.75
1994	$225,365.72	$5,945.53	$10,032.13	$35,856.27	$6,858.62
1995	$309,190.95	$6,271.94	$12,387.75	$43,083.53	$6,981.95
1996	$379,318.44	$6,585.90	$12,564.72	$45,148.35	$7,150.67
1997	$504,886.70	$6,919.20	$13,813.55	$50,491.61	$7,438.45
1998	$647,961.26	$7,249.71	$15,874.73	$54,503.40	$7,918.07
1999	$783,290.25	$7,585.98	$14,564.39	$54,962.95	$8,526.16
2000	$712,544.89	$8,027.23	$16,990.13	$60,090.82	$9,317.54
2001	$628,110.04	$8,299.22	$17,936.85	$64,789.41	$9,939.34
2002	$490,139.08	$8,432.21	$20,648.26	$72,679.38	$10,890.02
2003	$629,121.94	$8,517.45	$20,725.76	$82,514.37	$11,958.90
2004	$696,707.10	$8,634.28	$21,656.49	$90,673.91	$13,589.62
2005	$730,389.25	$8,905.97	$22,277.49	$95,132.83	$15,425.89
2006	$844,421.70	$9,326.93	$22,714.35	$101,838.17	$15,693.11
2007	$890,735.99	$9,732.96	$25,033.47	$105,046.46	$14,846.06
2008	$565,151.11	$9,865.81	$30,065.52	$99,725.11	$13,064.60
2009	$711,724.37	$9,880.61	$26,723.23	$122,990.48	$12,561.85
2010	$817,209.69	$9,894.12	$28,984.80	$133,257.53	$12,044.55
2011	$834,357.81	$9,899.31	$33,632.61	$150,027.35	$11,576.91
2012	$966,942.15	$9,907.81	$34,632.02	$165,217.13	$12,322.04
2013	$1,277,766.54	$9,913.59	$31,478.93	$163,472.60	$13,642.72
2014	$1,450,577.08	$9,916.81	$34,861.71	$180,449.08	$14,258.52
2015	$1,470,578.96	$9,922.02	$35,309.44	$179,190.42	$15,001.08
2016	$1,643,711.41	$9,953.52	$35,553.27	$197,763.69	$15,797.60
2017	$1,998,843.18	$10,046.17	$36,549.37	$216,994.04	$16,779.11
2018	$1,914,354.69	$10,240.98	$36,543.27	$210,999.30	$17,539.66
2019	$2,511,856.95	$10,399.72	$40,064.44	$243,344.35	$18,187.15
2020	$2,964,573.99	$10,409.08	$44,604.50	$268,680.24	$20,068.82
2021	$3,808,554.17	$10,415.32	$42,634.75	$271,188.22	$23,446.74

Table 1.3: Inflation rate from 1928

Year	Inflation Rate
1928	-1.16%
1929	0.58%

Year	Value
1930	-6.40%
1931	-9.32%
1932	-10.27%
1933	0.76%
1934	1.52%
1935	2.99%
1936	1.45%
1937	2.86%
1938	-2.78%
1939	0.00%
1940	0.71%
1941	9.93%
1942	9.03%
1943	2.96%
1944	2.30%
1945	2.25%
1946	18.13%
1947	8.84%
1948	2.99%
1949	-2.07%
1950	5.93%
1951	6.00%
1952	0.75%
1953	0.75%
1954	-0.74%
1955	0.37%
1956	2.99%
1957	2.90%
1958	1.76%
1959	1.73%
1960	1.36%
1961	0.67%
1962	1.33%
1963	1.64%
1964	0.97%
1965	1.92%
1966	3.46%
1967	3.04%
1968	4.72%
1969	6.20%
1970	5.57%
1971	3.27%
1972	3.41%
1973	8.71%
1974	12.34%
1975	6.94%

SO YOU WANT TO BE A SUPERINVESTOR?

Year	Rate
1976	4.86%
1977	6.70%
1978	9.02%
1979	13.29%
1980	12.52%
1981	8.92%
1982	3.83%
1983	3.79%
1984	3.95%
1985	3.80%
1986	1.10%
1987	4.43%
1988	4.42%
1989	4.65%
1990	6.11%
1991	3.06%
1992	2.90%
1993	2.75%
1994	2.67%
1995	2.54%
1996	3.32%
1997	1.70%
1998	1.61%
1999	2.68%
2000	3.39%
2001	1.55%
2002	2.38%
2003	1.88%
2004	3.26%
2005	3.42%
2006	2.54%
2007	4.08%
2008	0.09%
2009	2.72%
2010	1.50%
2011	2.96%
2012	1.74%
2013	1.50%
2014	0.76%
2015	0.73%
2016	2.07%
2017	2.11%
2018	1.91%
2019	2.29%
2020	1.36%
2021	7.00%

Table 1.4: Real returns for investments in S&P 500, 3-month T-Bills, US T-Bonds, Baa corporate bonds, and real estate from 1928

Year	S&P 500 (includes dividends)	3-month T- Bill	US T-Bonds	Baa Corp Bonds	Real Estate
1928	45.49%	4.29%	2.01%	4.43%	2.68%
1929	-8.83%	2.56%	3.60%	2.42%	-2.63%
1930	-20.01%	11.69%	11.68%	7.41%	2.24%
1931	-38.07%	12.82%	7.45%	-7.02%	1.29%
1932	1.82%	12.64%	21.25%	37.74%	-0.21%
1933	48.85%	0.20%	1.08%	12.11%	-4.54%
1934	-2.66%	-1.22%	6.35%	17.04%	1.37%
1935	42.49%	-2.74%	1.44%	10.02%	6.58%
1936	30.06%	-1.26%	3.52%	9.79%	1.74%
1937	-37.13%	-2.51%	-1.44%	-7.07%	-0.29%
1938	32.98%	2.92%	7.19%	12.36%	1.96%
1939	-1.10%	0.05%	4.41%	7.98%	-1.30%
1940	-11.31%	-0.67%	4.65%	7.88%	2.57%
1941	-20.65%	-8.91%	-10.87%	-4.48%	-16.66%
1942	9.30%	-7.97%	-6.18%	-3.53%	-5.23%
1943	21.47%	-2.50%	-0.46%	4.94%	8.24%
1944	16.36%	-1.88%	0.27%	4.17%	13.96%
1945	32.84%	-1.83%	1.52%	4.45%	9.32%
1946	-22.48%	-15.03%	-12.70%	-13.23%	5.05%
1947	-3.34%	-7.57%	-7.27%	-7.88%	11.42%
1948	2.63%	-1.89%	-1.01%	0.43%	-0.91%
1949	20.81%	3.26%	6.88%	7.61%	2.21%
1950	23.48%	-4.46%	-5.19%	-1.60%	-2.16%
1951	16.68%	-4.23%	-5.94%	-5.84%	0.04%
1952	17.27%	0.96%	1.50%	3.66%	3.62%
1953	-1.94%	1.13%	3.37%	0.86%	10.69%
1954	53.71%	1.69%	4.06%	6.95%	1.68%
1955	32.10%	1.35%	-1.70%	1.66%	-0.37%
1956	4.33%	-0.35%	-5.09%	-5.18%	-2.01%
1957	-12.98%	0.32%	3.79%	-3.52%	-0.18%
1958	41.23%	0.01%	-3.79%	4.59%	-1.08%
1959	10.15%	1.63%	-4.30%	-0.15%	-1.59%
1960	-1.01%	1.50%	10.14%	5.23%	-0.59%
1961	25.79%	1.67%	1.38%	4.40%	0.30%
1962	-10.01%	1.42%	4.30%	5.09%	-1.00%
1963	20.63%	1.49%	0.04%	3.76%	0.49%
1964	15.30%	2.55%	2.73%	4.15%	0.29%

SO YOU WANT TO BE A SUPERINVESTOR?

1965	10.28%	1.99%	-1.18%	1.24%	-0.26%
1966	-12.98%	1.36%	-0.53%	-6.67%	-2.16%
1967	20.15%	1.23%	-4.48%	-2.08%	-0.70%
1968	5.82%	0.59%	-1.38%	0.12%	-0.56%
1969	-13.60%	0.44%	-10.56%	-7.74%	0.75%
1970	-1.90%	0.78%	10.59%	0.08%	2.51%
1971	10.61%	1.03%	6.31%	10.40%	0.95%
1972	14.84%	0.64%	-0.57%	7.74%	-0.42%
1973	-21.17%	-1.54%	-4.64%	-4.04%	-4.86%
1974	-34.04%	-4.01%	-9.21%	-14.88%	-2.02%
1975	28.11%	-1.09%	-3.12%	3.85%	-0.15%
1976	18.09%	0.10%	10.60%	14.20%	3.16%
1977	-12.82%	-1.34%	-5.07%	3.05%	7.45%
1978	-2.30%	-1.68%	-8.99%	-5.39%	6.15%
1979	4.61%	-2.85%	-11.14%	-13.51%	0.40%
1980	17.08%	-0.96%	-13.78%	-14.07%	-4.55%
1981	-12.51%	4.68%	-0.66%	-0.42%	-3.51%
1982	15.98%	6.53%	27.92%	24.29%	-3.15%
1983	17.87%	4.64%	-0.57%	11.95%	0.92%
1984	2.11%	5.36%	9.41%	11.23%	0.70%
1985	26.43%	3.55%	21.11%	19.33%	3.54%
1986	17.21%	4.83%	22.93%	20.17%	8.42%
1987	1.32%	1.28%	-9.00%	-2.05%	3.30%
1988	11.60%	2.15%	3.64%	10.24%	2.67%
1989	25.64%	3.31%	12.47%	10.65%	-0.25%
1990	-8.64%	1.31%	0.12%	0.03%	-6.41%
1991	26.36%	2.24%	11.59%	14.35%	-3.13%
1992	4.46%	0.52%	6.28%	9.01%	-2.02%
1993	7.03%	0.24%	11.16%	13.32%	-0.57%
1994	-1.31%	1.53%	-10.43%	-3.89%	-0.16%
1995	33.80%	2.88%	20.42%	17.18%	-0.72%
1996	18.74%	1.63%	-1.83%	1.42%	-0.88%
1997	30.88%	3.30%	8.10%	9.96%	2.28%
1998	26.30%	3.11%	13.10%	6.23%	4.76%
1999	17.72%	1.90%	-10.65%	-1.79%	4.86%
2000	-12.01%	2.35%	12.83%	5.75%	5.70%
2001	-13.20%	1.81%	3.96%	6.17%	5.04%
2002	-23.78%	-0.76%	12.44%	9.57%	7.02%
2003	25.99%	-0.85%	-1.48%	11.44%	7.79%
2004	7.25%	-1.82%	1.20%	6.42%	10.05%
2005	1.37%	-0.26%	-0.53%	1.45%	9.76%
2006	12.75%	2.13%	-0.57%	4.40%	-0.79%
2007	1.35%	0.26%	5.89%	-0.89%	-9.11%
2008	-36.61%	1.27%	19.99%	-5.15%	-12.08%
2009	22.60%	-2.50%	-13.47%	20.06%	-6.40%
2010	13.13%	-1.34%	6.86%	6.75%	-5.53%

2011	-0.84%	-2.83%	12.70%	9.35%	-6.65%
2012	13.91%	-1.63%	1.21%	8.24%	4.61%
2013	30.19%	-1.42%	-10.45%	-2.52%	9.08%
2014	12.67%	-0.72%	9.91%	9.56%	3.73%
2015	0.64%	-0.67%	0.55%	-1.42%	4.45%
2016	9.50%	-1.72%	-1.36%	8.12%	3.17%
2017	19.09%	-1.15%	0.68%	7.46%	4.02%
2018	-6.02%	0.03%	-1.89%	-4.59%	2.57%
2019	28.28%	-0.72%	7.19%	12.75%	1.38%
2020	16.44%	-1.25%	9.84%	8.93%	8.86%
2021	20.06%	-6.49%	-10.67%	-5.67%	9.19%

Table 1.5: Real value of $500 invested in S&P 500, 3-month T-Bills, US T-Bonds, Baa corporate bonds, and real estate from 1928

Year	S&P 500 (includes dividends)	3-month T-Bill	US T-Bond	Baa Corporate Bond	Real Estate
1928	$727.47	$521.43	$510.07	$522.13	$513.39
1929	$663.22	$534.78	$528.43	$534.76	$499.91
1930	$530.53	$597.31	$590.17	$574.38	$511.10
1931	$328.57	$673.89	$634.15	$534.08	$517.67
1932	$334.54	$759.09	$768.88	$735.64	$516.56
1933	$497.95	$760.57	$777.22	$824.73	$493.11
1934	$484.69	$751.31	$826.58	$965.29	$499.86
1935	$690.62	$730.75	$838.52	$1,062.05	$532.77
1936	$898.21	$721.56	$868.02	$1,166.05	$542.07
1937	$564.68	$703.45	$855.54	$1,083.60	$540.52
1938	$750.89	$724.02	$917.06	$1,217.50	$551.10
1939	$742.65	$724.35	$957.53	$1,314.69	$543.93
1940	$658.68	$719.47	$1,002.10	$1,418.26	$557.93
1941	$522.66	$655.33	$893.15	$1,354.76	$464.98
1942	$571.28	$603.10	$837.96	$1,306.89	$440.68
1943	$693.92	$588.00	$834.15	$1,371.45	$477.01
1944	$807.42	$576.97	$836.42	$1,428.66	$543.62
1945	$1,072.54	$566.43	$849.16	$1,492.27	$594.29
1946	$831.39	$481.31	$741.31	$1,294.90	$624.32
1947	$803.60	$444.89	$687.38	$1,192.88	$695.60
1948	$824.77	$436.48	$680.44	$1,198.04	$689.30
1949	$996.40	$450.70	$727.26	$1,289.21	$704.53
1950	$1,230.36	$430.58	$689.48	$1,268.60	$689.29
1951	$1,435.56	$412.37	$648.53	$1,194.51	$689.60
1952	$1,683.43	$416.33	$658.28	$1,238.21	$714.60

SO YOU WANT TO BE A SUPERINVESTOR?

1953	$1,650.72	$421.05	$680.46	$1,248.92	$790.97
1954	$2,537.26	$428.18	$708.11	$1,335.76	$804.25
1955	$3,351.79	$433.94	$696.04	$1,357.98	$801.24
1956	$3,496.76	$432.44	$660.62	$1,287.60	$785.13
1957	$3,042.89	$433.81	$685.64	$1,242.33	$783.76
1958	$4,297.58	$433.85	$659.64	$1,299.34	$775.29
1959	$4,733.82	$440.91	$631.26	$1,297.35	$762.94
1960	$4,686.00	$447.54	$695.28	$1,365.22	$758.46
1961	$5,894.68	$455.02	$704.87	$1,425.28	$760.77
1962	$5,304.54	$461.49	$735.20	$1,497.89	$753.18
1963	$6,398.76	$468.36	$735.49	$1,554.18	$756.88
1964	$7,377.52	$480.31	$755.57	$1,618.68	$759.04
1965	$8,135.82	$489.86	$746.64	$1,638.80	$757.07
1966	$7,079.70	$496.50	$742.67	$1,529.44	$740.71
1967	$8,506.33	$502.61	$709.37	$1,497.61	$735.51
1968	$9,001.43	$505.58	$699.58	$1,499.40	$731.39
1969	$7,777.60	$507.81	$625.72	$1,383.31	$736.88
1970	$7,629.58	$511.76	$692.01	$1,384.35	$755.34
1971	$8,438.95	$517.05	$735.71	$1,528.26	$762.50
1972	$9,691.58	$520.38	$731.53	$1,646.53	$759.33
1973	$7,639.79	$512.36	$697.56	$1,580.07	$722.42
1974	$5,039.23	$491.81	$633.30	$1,344.92	$707.86
1975	$6,455.70	$486.46	$613.57	$1,396.66	$706.78
1976	$7,623.30	$486.97	$678.63	$1,594.95	$729.11
1977	$6,645.87	$480.44	$644.22	$1,643.58	$783.46
1978	$6,492.96	$472.37	$586.34	$1,554.93	$831.65
1979	$6,792.44	$458.93	$521.01	$1,344.90	$834.95
1980	$7,952.65	$454.51	$449.21	$1,155.66	$796.96
1981	$6,957.88	$475.81	$446.22	$1,150.78	$768.95
1982	$8,069.57	$506.90	$570.79	$1,430.33	$744.76
1983	$9,511.50	$530.44	$567.54	$1,601.26	$751.64
1984	$9,712.57	$558.88	$620.96	$1,781.04	$756.92
1985	$12,279.84	$578.70	$752.06	$2,125.31	$783.70
1986	$14,392.93	$606.63	$924.54	$2,553.90	$849.70
1987	$14,582.88	$614.42	$841.37	$2,501.46	$877.70
1988	$16,275.22	$627.65	$872.02	$2,757.68	$901.17
1989	$20,447.61	$648.43	$980.74	$3,051.31	$898.88
1990	$18,680.33	$656.90	$981.93	$3,052.28	$841.29
1991	$23,604.98	$671.63	$1,095.69	$3,490.26	$814.99
1992	$24,658.61	$675.10	$1,164.49	$3,804.75	$798.49
1993	$26,391.01	$676.73	$1,294.40	$4,311.43	$793.90
1994	$26,044.28	$687.09	$1,159.36	$4,143.71	$792.61
1995	$34,846.94	$706.87	$1,396.14	$4,855.67	$786.89
1996	$41,375.86	$718.39	$1,370.55	$4,924.76	$779.99
1997	$54,150.92	$742.11	$1,481.55	$5,415.41	$797.80
1998	$68,393.74	$765.22	$1,675.61	$5,752.95	$835.77

1999	$80,516.50	$779.78	$1,497.11	$5,649.79	$876.43
2000	$70,845.01	$798.11	$1,689.25	$5,974.55	$926.40
2001	$61,495.80	$812.54	$1,756.13	$6,343.28	$973.12
2002	$46,873.46	$806.40	$1,974.65	$6,950.55	$1,041.45
2003	$59,054.88	$799.52	$1,945.50	$7,745.52	$1,122.57
2004	$63,337.04	$784.93	$1,968.77	$8,243.09	$1,235.42
2005	$64,205.99	$782.89	$1,958.34	$8,362.80	$1,356.04
2006	$72,390.99	$799.58	$1,947.27	$8,730.43	$1,345.35
2007	$73,367.13	$801.67	$2,061.93	$8,652.35	$1,222.82
2008	$46,507.21	$811.87	$2,474.14	$8,206.54	$1,075.11
2009	$57,017.34	$791.55	$2,140.84	$9,852.96	$1,006.35
2010	$64,503.14	$780.95	$2,287.80	$10,518.14	$950.69
2011	$63,961.84	$758.88	$2,578.27	$11,501.09	$887.49
2012	$72,857.29	$746.53	$2,609.46	$12,448.80	$928.44
2013	$94,852.89	$735.92	$2,336.79	$12,135.12	$1,012.74
2014	$106,872.71	$730.63	$2,568.47	$13,294.77	$1,050.51
2015	$107,561.69	$725.72	$2,582.62	$13,106.42	$1,097.22
2016	$117,781.50	$713.23	$2,547.60	$14,170.92	$1,131.99
2017	$140,270.34	$705.00	$2,564.88	$15,227.72	$1,177.49
2018	$131,823.26	$705.20	$2,516.38	$14,529.50	$1,207.79
2019	$169,103.29	$700.13	$2,697.22	$16,382.43	$1,224.40
2020	$196,899.32	$691.34	$2,962.52	$17,845.05	$1,332.92
2021	$236,405.89	$646.50	$2,646.44	$16,833.29	$1,455.39

Table 2.1: Annual returns for investments in S&P 500 and gold from 1969 to 2021

Year	S&P 500 (includes dividends)	Gold
1969	-8.24%	-16.07%
1970	3.56%	6.16%
1971	14.22%	16.37%
1972	18.76%	48.74%
1973	-14.31%	73.49%
1974	-25.90%	67.04%
1975	37.00%	-25.20%
1976	23.83%	-4.06%
1977	-6.98%	23.08%
1978	6.51%	35.57%
1979	18.52%	133.41%
1980	31.74%	12.50%
1981	-4.70%	-32.15%
1982	20.42%	12.00%
1983	22.34%	-14.84%
1984	6.15%	-19.00%

1985	31.24%	5.83%
1986	18.49%	19.54%
1987	5.81%	24.46%
1988	16.54%	-15.69%
1989	31.48%	-2.23%
1990	-3.06%	-2.49%
1991	30.23%	-9.62%
1992	7.49%	-5.80%
1993	9.97%	17.35%
1994	1.33%	-2.09%
1995	37.20%	1.10%
1996	22.68%	-4.43%
1997	33.10%	-21.74%
1998	28.34%	-0.61%
1999	20.89%	1.18%
2000	-9.03%	-6.26%
2001	-11.85%	1.41%
2002	-21.97%	23.96%
2003	28.36%	21.74%
2004	10.74%	4.97%
2005	4.83%	17.12%
2006	15.61%	23.92%
2007	5.48%	31.59%
2008	-36.55%	27.63%
2009	25.94%	27.74%
2010	14.82%	11.65%
2011	2.10%	5.68%
2012	15.89%	-27.79%
2013	32.15%	-0.19%
2014	13.52%	-11.59%
2015	1.38%	8.63%
2016	11.77%	12.57%
2017	21.61%	-1.15%
2018	-4.23%	18.83%
2019	31.21%	24.43%
2020	18.02%	-3.51%
2021	28.47%	-1.12%

Table 2.2: Nominal value of $500 invested in S&P 500 and gold from 1969 to 2021

Year	S&P 500 (includes dividends)	Gold
1969	$458.79	$419.65
1970	$475.13	$445.50

1971	$542.70	$518.43
1972	$644.49	$771.11
1973	$552.27	$1,337.80
1974	$409.22	$2,234.66
1975	$560.62	$1,671.53
1976	$694.22	$1,603.66
1977	$645.76	$1,973.79
1978	$687.80	$2,675.87
1979	$815.17	$6,245.74
1980	$1,073.87	$7,026.45
1981	$1,023.37	$4,767.45
1982	$1,232.34	$5,339.54
1983	$1,507.61	$4,547.16
1984	$1,600.27	$3,683.20
1985	$2,100.11	$3,897.93
1986	$2,488.52	$4,659.58
1987	$2,633.17	$5,799.31
1988	$3,068.62	$4,889.40
1989	$4,034.48	$4,780.37
1990	$3,910.84	$4,661.34
1991	$5,093.28	$4,212.92
1992	$5,474.96	$3,968.57
1993	$6,020.65	$4,657.11
1994	$6,100.48	$4,559.78
1995	$8,369.57	$4,609.94
1996	$10,267.86	$4,405.72
1997	$13,666.90	$3,447.91
1998	$17,539.82	$3,426.88
1999	$21,203.08	$3,467.32
2000	$19,288.05	$3,250.27
2001	$17,002.46	$3,296.09
2002	$13,267.69	$4,085.84
2003	$17,029.86	$4,974.10
2004	$18,859.33	$5,221.31
2005	$19,771.09	$6,115.20
2006	$22,857.86	$7,577.96
2007	$24,111.55	$9,971.83
2008	$15,298.21	$12,727.05
2009	$19,265.84	$16,257.53
2010	$22,121.25	$18,151.54
2011	$22,585.44	$19,182.54
2012	$26,174.39	$13,851.72
2013	$34,588.17	$13,825.40
2014	$39,266.03	$12,223.03
2015	$39,807.46	$13,277.88
2016	$44,494.03	$14,946.91

2017	$54,107.17	$14,775.02
2018	$51,820.14	$17,557.16
2019	$67,994.07	$21,846.37
2020	$80,248.78	$21,079.56
2021	$103,094.68	$20,843.47

Table 2.3: Real returns for investments in S&P 500 and gold from 1969 to 2021

Year	S&P 500 (includes dividends)	Gold
1969	-13.60%	-20.97%
1970	-1.90%	0.56%
1971	10.61%	12.69%
1972	14.84%	43.84%
1973	-21.17%	59.60%
1974	-34.04%	48.69%
1975	28.11%	-30.05%
1976	18.09%	-8.51%
1977	-12.82%	15.35%
1978	-2.30%	24.36%
1979	4.61%	106.02%
1980	17.08%	-0.01%
1981	-12.51%	-37.71%
1982	15.98%	7.87%
1983	17.87%	-17.95%
1984	2.11%	-22.08%
1985	26.43%	1.96%
1986	17.21%	18.24%
1987	1.32%	19.18%
1988	11.60%	-19.26%
1989	25.64%	-6.57%
1990	-8.64%	-8.10%
1991	26.36%	-12.31%
1992	4.46%	-8.46%
1993	7.03%	14.21%
1994	-1.31%	-4.64%
1995	33.80%	-1.40%
1996	18.74%	-7.50%
1997	30.88%	-23.05%
1998	26.30%	-2.19%
1999	17.72%	-1.47%
2000	-12.01%	-9.33%
2001	-13.20%	-0.14%
2002	-23.78%	21.08%

2003	25.99%	19.49%
2004	7.25%	1.66%
2005	1.37%	13.25%
2006	12.75%	20.85%
2007	1.35%	26.43%
2008	-36.61%	27.51%
2009	22.60%	24.36%
2010	13.13%	10.00%
2011	-0.84%	2.64%
2012	13.91%	-29.03%
2013	30.19%	-1.67%
2014	12.67%	-12.25%
2015	0.64%	7.84%
2016	9.50%	10.28%
2017	19.09%	-3.19%
2018	-6.02%	16.60%
2019	28.28%	21.65%
2020	16.44%	-4.81%
2021	20.06%	-7.59%

Table 2.4: Real value of $500 invested in S&P 500 and gold from 1969 to 2021

Year	S&P 500 (includes dividends)	Gold
1969	$432.02	$395.16
1970	$423.80	$397.37
1971	$468.76	$447.79
1972	$538.34	$644.10
1973	$424.37	$1,027.96
1974	$279.91	$1,528.53
1975	$358.59	$1,069.18
1976	$423.45	$978.18
1977	$369.16	$1,128.33
1978	$360.66	$1,403.15
1979	$377.30	$2,890.79
1980	$441.74	$2,890.37
1981	$386.49	$1,800.47
1982	$448.24	$1,942.15
1983	$528.33	$1,593.52
1984	$539.50	$1,241.72
1985	$682.10	$1,266.02
1986	$799.48	$1,496.97
1987	$810.03	$1,784.02
1988	$904.03	$1,440.45

Year		
1989	$1,135.80	$1,345.78
1990	$1,037.63	$1,236.75
1991	$1,311.18	$1,084.54
1992	$1,369.70	$992.84
1993	$1,465.93	$1,133.93
1994	$1,446.67	$1,081.31
1995	$1,935.63	$1,066.14
1996	$2,298.29	$986.15
1997	$3,007.90	$758.84
1998	$3,799.05	$742.25
1999	$4,472.43	$731.37
2000	$3,935.21	$663.13
2001	$3,415.89	$662.20
2002	$2,603.67	$801.81
2003	$3,280.30	$958.11
2004	$3,518.16	$974.02
2005	$3,566.43	$1,103.10
2006	$4,021.08	$1,333.09
2007	$4,075.30	$1,685.43
2008	$2,583.32	$2,149.14
2009	$3,167.13	$2,672.59
2010	$3,582.94	$2,939.97
2011	$3,552.87	$3,017.57
2012	$4,046.98	$2,141.70
2013	$5,268.77	$2,106.00
2014	$5,936.43	$1,847.94
2015	$5,974.70	$1,992.88
2016	$6,542.37	$2,197.78
2017	$7,791.56	$2,127.64
2018	$7,322.35	$2,480.88
2019	$9,393.13	$3,018.00
2020	$10,937.11	$2,872.93
2021	$13,131.57	$2,654.91

Table 3.1: Annual returns for investments in S&P 500, 3-month T-Bills, US T-Bonds, Baa corporate bonds, real estate, and gold from 1991 to 2021

Year	S&P 500 (includes dividends)	3-month T-Bill	US T-Bond	Baa Corporate Bond	Real Estate	Gold
1991	30.23%	5.38%	15.00%	17.85%	-0.16%	-9.62%
1992	7.49%	3.43%	9.36%	12.17%	0.82%	-5.80%
1993	9.97%	3.00%	14.21%	16.43%	2.16%	17.35%

1994	1.33%	4.25%	-8.04%	-1.32%	2.51%	-2.09%
1995	37.20%	5.49%	23.48%	20.16%	1.80%	1.10%
1996	22.68%	5.01%	1.43%	4.79%	2.42%	-4.43%
1997	33.10%	5.06%	9.94%	11.83%	4.02%	-21.74%
1998	28.34%	4.78%	14.92%	7.95%	6.45%	-0.61%
1999	20.89%	4.64%	-8.25%	0.84%	7.68%	1.18%
2000	-9.03%	5.82%	16.66%	9.33%	9.28%	-6.26%
2001	-11.85%	3.39%	5.57%	7.82%	6.67%	1.41%
2002	-21.97%	1.60%	15.12%	12.18%	9.56%	23.96%
2003	28.36%	1.01%	0.38%	13.53%	9.82%	21.74%
2004	10.74%	1.37%	4.49%	9.89%	13.64%	4.97%
2005	4.83%	3.15%	2.87%	4.92%	13.51%	17.12%
2006	15.61%	4.73%	1.96%	7.05%	1.73%	23.92%
2007	5.48%	4.35%	10.21%	3.15%	-5.40%	31.59%
2008	-36.55%	1.37%	20.10%	-5.07%	-12.00%	27.63%
2009	25.94%	0.15%	-11.12%	23.33%	-3.85%	27.74%
2010	14.82%	0.14%	8.46%	8.35%	-4.12%	11.65%
2011	2.10%	0.05%	16.04%	12.58%	-3.88%	5.68%
2012	15.89%	0.09%	2.97%	10.12%	6.44%	-27.79%
2013	32.15%	0.06%	-9.10%	-1.06%	10.72%	-0.19%
2014	13.52%	0.03%	10.75%	10.38%	4.51%	-11.59%
2015	1.38%	0.05%	1.28%	-0.70%	5.21%	8.63%
2016	11.77%	0.32%	0.69%	10.37%	5.31%	12.57%
2017	21.61%	0.93%	2.80%	9.72%	6.21%	-1.15%
2018	-4.23%	1.94%	-0.02%	-2.76%	4.53%	18.83%
2019	31.21%	1.55%	9.64%	15.33%	3.69%	24.43%
2020	18.02%	0.09%	11.33%	10.41%	10.35%	-3.51%
2021	28.47%	0.06%	-4.42%	0.93%	16.83%	-1.12%

Table 3.2: Nominal value of $500 invested in S&P 500, 3-month T-Bills, US T-Bonds, Baa corporate bonds, real estate, and gold from 1991 to 2021

Year	S&P 500 (includes dividends)	3-month T- Bill	US T-Bonds	Baa Corp Bonds	Real Estate	Gold
1991	$651.17	$526.88	$575.02	$589.27	$499.21	$451.90
1992	$699.97	$544.96	$628.85	$660.99	$503.29	$425.69
1993	$769.74	$561.29	$718.22	$769.61	$514.15	$499.55
1994	$779.94	$585.13	$660.50	$759.45	$527.05	$489.11
1995	$1,070.05	$617.25	$815.59	$912.53	$536.53	$494.49
1996	$1,312.74	$648.15	$827.24	$956.26	$549.49	$472.58
1997	$1,747.31	$680.95	$909.46	$1,069.44	$571.61	$369.84
1998	$2,242.46	$713.48	$1,045.17	$1,154.41	$608.46	$367.59

Year						
1999	$2,710.81	$746.57	$958.90	$1,164.14	$655.19	$371.92
2000	$2,465.97	$790.00	$1,118.60	$1,272.75	$716.01	$348.64
2001	$2,173.76	$816.76	$1,180.93	$1,372.27	$763.79	$353.56
2002	$1,696.27	$829.85	$1,359.45	$1,539.39	$836.84	$438.27
2003	$2,177.26	$838.24	$1,364.55	$1,747.69	$918.98	$533.55
2004	$2,411.16	$849.74	$1,425.83	$1,920.52	$1,044.29	$560.07
2005	$2,527.73	$876.48	$1,466.71	$2,014.96	$1,185.40	$655.95
2006	$2,922.37	$917.91	$1,495.48	$2,156.98	$1,205.94	$812.85
2007	$3,082.65	$957.86	$1,648.16	$2,224.94	$1,140.85	$1,069.63
2008	$1,955.87	$970.94	$1,979.47	$2,112.23	$1,003.95	$1,365.17
2009	$2,463.13	$972.40	$1,759.41	$2,605.00	$965.32	$1,743.87
2010	$2,828.19	$973.73	$1,908.31	$2,822.46	$925.56	$1,947.03
2011	$2,887.54	$974.24	$2,214.32	$3,177.65	$889.63	$2,057.62
2012	$3,346.39	$975.07	$2,280.12	$3,499.38	$946.89	$1,485.81
2013	$4,422.09	$975.64	$2,072.52	$3,462.43	$1,048.37	$1,482.99
2014	$5,020.15	$975.96	$2,295.24	$3,822.00	$1,095.70	$1,311.11
2015	$5,089.37	$976.47	$2,324.72	$3,795.34	$1,152.76	$1,424.26
2016	$5,688.54	$979.57	$2,340.77	$4,188.73	$1,213.97	$1,603.29
2017	$6,917.58	$988.69	$2,406.35	$4,596.04	$1,289.39	$1,584.85
2018	$6,625.18	$1,007.86	$2,405.95	$4,469.07	$1,347.83	$1,883.27
2019	$8,693.02	$1,023.48	$2,637.78	$5,154.15	$1,397.59	$2,343.36
2020	$10,259.78	$1,024.40	$2,936.69	$5,690.78	$1,542.19	$2,261.11
2021	$13,180.62	$1,025.02	$2,807.00	$5,743.90	$1,801.76	$2,235.78

Table 3.3: Real returns for investments in S&P 500, 3-month T-Bills, US T-Bonds, Baa corporate bonds, real estate, and gold from 1991 to 2021

Year	S&P 500 (includes dividends)	3-month T-Bills	US T-Bonds	Baa Corp Bonds	Real Estate	Gold
1991	26.36%	2.24%	11.59%	14.35%	-3.13%	-12.31%
1992	4.46%	0.52%	6.28%	9.01%	-2.02%	-8.46%
1993	7.03%	0.24%	11.16%	13.32%	-0.57%	14.21%
1994	-1.31%	1.53%	-10.43%	-3.89%	-0.16%	-4.64%
1995	33.80%	2.88%	20.42%	17.18%	-0.72%	-1.40%
1996	18.74%	1.63%	-1.83%	1.42%	-0.88%	-7.50%
1997	30.88%	3.30%	8.10%	9.96%	2.28%	-23.05%
1998	26.30%	3.11%	13.10%	6.23%	4.76%	-2.19%
1999	17.72%	1.90%	-10.65%	-1.79%	4.86%	-1.47%
2000	-12.01%	2.35%	12.83%	5.75%	5.70%	-9.33%
2001	-13.20%	1.81%	3.96%	6.17%	5.04%	-0.14%
2002	-23.78%	-0.76%	12.44%	9.57%	7.02%	21.08%
2003	25.99%	-0.85%	-1.48%	11.44%	7.79%	19.49%

2004	7.25%	-1.82%	1.20%	6.42%	10.05%	1.66%
2005	1.37%	-0.26%	-0.53%	1.45%	9.76%	13.25%
2006	12.75%	2.13%	-0.57%	4.40%	-0.79%	20.85%
2007	1.35%	0.26%	5.89%	-0.89%	-9.11%	26.43%
2008	-36.61%	1.27%	19.99%	-5.15%	-12.08%	27.51%
2009	22.60%	-2.50%	-13.47%	20.06%	-6.40%	24.36%
2010	13.13%	-1.34%	6.86%	6.75%	-5.53%	10.00%
2011	-0.84%	-2.83%	12.70%	9.35%	-6.65%	2.64%
2012	13.91%	-1.63%	1.21%	8.24%	4.61%	-29.03%
2013	30.19%	-1.42%	-10.45%	-2.52%	9.08%	-1.67%
2014	12.67%	-0.72%	9.91%	9.56%	3.73%	-12.25%
2015	0.64%	-0.67%	0.55%	-1.42%	4.45%	7.84%
2016	9.50%	-1.72%	-1.36%	8.12%	3.17%	10.28%
2017	19.09%	-1.15%	0.68%	7.46%	4.02%	-3.19%
2018	-6.02%	0.03%	-1.89%	-4.59%	2.57%	16.60%
2019	28.28%	-0.72%	7.19%	12.75%	1.38%	21.65%
2020	16.44%	-1.25%	9.84%	8.93%	8.86%	-4.81%
2021	20.06%	-6.49%	-10.67%	-5.67%	9.19%	-7.59%

Table 3.4: Real value of $500 invested in S&P 500, 3-month T-Bills, US T-Bonds, Baa corporate bonds, real estate, and gold from 1991 to 2021

Year	S&P 500 (includes dividends)	3-month T-Bill	US T-Bonds	Baa Corp Bonds	Real Estate	Gold
1991	$631.81	$511.21	$557.93	$571.75	$484.37	$438.46
1992	$660.02	$513.85	$592.96	$623.26	$474.56	$401.39
1993	$706.39	$515.09	$659.11	$706.26	$471.83	$458.43
1994	$697.10	$522.98	$590.35	$678.79	$471.07	$437.16
1995	$932.72	$538.03	$710.92	$795.42	$467.67	$431.02
1996	$1,107.47	$546.80	$697.89	$806.73	$463.57	$398.68
1997	$1,449.41	$564.86	$754.41	$887.11	$474.15	$306.79
1998	$1,830.64	$582.45	$853.22	$942.40	$496.72	$300.08
1999	$2,155.11	$593.53	$762.33	$925.50	$520.88	$295.68
2000	$1,896.25	$607.48	$860.17	$978.70	$550.58	$268.09
2001	$1,646.00	$618.47	$894.22	$1,039.11	$578.35	$267.72
2002	$1,254.62	$613.79	$1,005.50	$1,138.58	$618.96	$324.16
2003	$1,580.67	$608.55	$990.65	$1,268.81	$667.17	$387.35
2004	$1,695.29	$597.45	$1,002.50	$1,350.32	$734.24	$393.78
2005	$1,718.55	$595.90	$997.19	$1,369.93	$805.93	$445.97
2006	$1,937.63	$608.60	$991.55	$1,430.15	$799.58	$538.95
2007	$1,963.75	$610.19	$1,049.94	$1,417.36	$726.76	$681.39
2008	$1,244.82	$617.96	$1,259.83	$1,344.33	$638.97	$868.87

SO YOU WANT TO BE A SUPERINVESTOR?

2009	$1,526.13	$602.49	$1,090.12	$1,614.03	$598.10	$1,080.49
2010	$1,726.50	$594.42	$1,164.95	$1,723.00	$565.02	$1,188.58
2011	$1,712.01	$577.62	$1,312.86	$1,884.02	$527.46	$1,219.96
2012	$1,950.11	$568.22	$1,328.74	$2,039.26	$551.80	$865.86
2013	$2,538.84	$560.14	$1,189.89	$1,987.88	$601.90	$851.42
2014	$2,860.57	$556.12	$1,307.87	$2,177.84	$624.35	$747.09
2015	$2,879.01	$552.38	$1,315.07	$2,146.99	$652.10	$805.69
2016	$3,152.55	$542.87	$1,297.24	$2,321.37	$672.77	$888.53
2017	$3,754.49	$536.61	$1,306.04	$2,494.48	$699.81	$860.17
2018	$3,528.40	$536.76	$1,281.35	$2,380.11	$717.82	$1,002.98
2019	$4,526.24	$532.90	$1,373.43	$2,683.64	$727.69	$1,220.13
2020	$5,270.23	$526.22	$1,508.52	$2,923.23	$792.19	$1,161.48
2021	$6,327.67	$492.08	$1,347.57	$2,757.50	$864.98	$1,073.34

APPENDIX 2
Sources

Berardino, M. 2012. "Mike Tyson Explains One of His Most Famous Quotes." *Sun Sentinel*. Retrieved September 20, 2022. https://www.sun-sentinel.com/sports/fl-xpm-2012-11-09-sfl-mike-tyson-explains-one-of-his-most-famous-quotes-20121109-story.html.

Bernhardt, D., and Eckblad, M. 2013. "Stock Market Crash of 1987." Federal Reserve History. Retrieved September 15, 2022. https://www.federalreservehistory.org/essays/stock-market-crash-of-1987.

Booth, D. D. M., and J. V. Duca. 2007. "The Rise and Fall of Subprime Mortgages, Volume 2, Number 11." November 1. FRASER. Retrieved February 11, 2023. https://fraser.stlouisfed.org/title/economic-letter-6362/rise-fall-subprime-mortgages-607610.

Brooks, J. 1999. *Once in Golconda: A True Drama of Wall Street, 1920–1938*. John Wiley.

Browne, C. 2000. *Value Investing and Behavioral Finance*. November 15. Tweedy, Browne Company LLC. Established 1920. https://www.tweedy.com/resources/library_docs/papers/ChrisBrowneColumbiaSpeech2000.pdf.

Buffet, M., and Clark, D. 2002. *The New Buffettology*. Simon & Schuster.

Buffett, W. E. 1982. "*Chairman's Letter—1981.*" Berkshire Hathaway. February 6. *https://www.berkshirehathaway.com/letters/1981.html*.

Buffett, W. E. 1984. "The Superinvestors of Graham-and-Doddsville." Reprinted from *Hermes*, the Columbia Business School Magazine. *https://www8.gsb.columbia.edu/sites/valueinvesting/files/files/Buffett1984.pdf*.

Buffett, W. E. 1986. "Chairman's Letter—1986." Berkshire Hathaway. https://www.berkshirehathaway.com/letters/1986.html.

Buffett, W. E. 1988. "Chairman's Letter—1987." Berkshire Hathaway. February 28. https://www.berkshirehathaway.com/letters/1987.html.

Buffett, W. E. 1988. "Chairman's Letter—1988." Berkshire Hathaway. February 24. https://www.berkshirehathaway.com/letters/1988.html.

Buffett, W. E. 1990. "Chairman's Letter—1989." Berkshire Hathaway. March 2. https://www.berkshirehathaway.com/letters/1989.html.

Buffett, W. E. 1998. "Chairman's Letter—1997." Berkshire Hathaway. February 27. https://www.berkshirehathaway.com/letters/1997.html.

Buffett W. E. 2003. "Chairman's Letter—2002." Berkshire Hathaway. February 21. https://www.berkshirehathaway.com/letters/2002pdf.pdf.

Buffett, W. E. 2008. "Chairman's Letter—2007." Berkshire Hathaway. February. https://www.berkshirehathaway.com/letters/2007ltr.pdf.

Buffett, W. E. 2015. "Chairman's Letter—2014." Berkshire Hathaway. February 27. https://www.berkshirehathaway.com/letters/2014ltr.pdf.

Buffett, W. E. 2018. "Chairman's Letter—2017." Berkshire Hathaway. February 24. https://www.berkshirehathaway.com/letters/2017ltr.pdf.

Buffett, Warren. n.d. "If you don't find a way to make money while you sleep, you will work until you die." Quotefancy. Retrieved September 13, 2022. https://quotefancy.com/quote/930999/Warren-Buffett-If-you-don-t-find-a-way-to-make-money-while-you-sleep-you-will-work-until.

Buffett, W. E., and Munger C. 2018. "Berkshire Hathaway Annual Meeting 2018." Edited transcript provided by CNBC. https://s3.amazonaws.com/static.contentres.com/media/documents/e3ab342f-baae-465d-a5d3-41a789b624cb.pdf.

Forbes. 2013. "Warren Buffett—in 1974." *Forbes* magazine. June 19. Retrieved September 20, 2022. https://www.forbes.com/2008/04/30/warren-buffett-profile-invest-oped-cx_hs_0430buffett.html.

Forsyth, R. W. 2022. "The Case for Building Wealth with Stocks, Not Homes." *Barron's*. April 1. Retrieved September 17, 2022. https://www.barrons.com/articles/stocks-housing-wealth-51648766521.

Graham B. 2003. *The Intelligent Investor* revised edition. HarperCollins Publishers Inc.

Grantham, J. 2012. "Advice from Uncle Polonius." GMO. https://realinvestmentadvice.com/pdf_converter/htmltopdf.php?Tboto=407428&dfTitle=investing-advice-from-uncle-polonius-illustrated.

Greenblatt, J. 1997. "You can be a stock market genius (even if you're not too smart): uncover the secret hiding places of stock market profits." Simon & Schuster Inc.

Hagstrom, R. G. 2000. *The Warren Buffett Portfolio: Mastering the Power of the Focus Investment Strategy*. Wiley.

Hagstrom, R. G. 2014. *The Warren Buffett Way*. Wiley.

Hargreaves, R. 2020. "Case Study: The Fall of Rick Guerin." Yahoo Finance taken from GuruFocus.com. December 16. https://www.yahoo.com/video/case-study-fall-rick-guerin170021290.html.

Housel, M. 2020. *The Psychology of Money: Timeless Lessons on Wealth, Greed, and Happiness*. Harriman House.

Investment Masters Class. n.d. "Compounding." Retrieved September 16, 2022. http://mastersinvest.com/compounding.

Investment Masters Class. n.d. "Diversification." Retrieved September 18, 2022. http://mastersinvest.com/diversificationquotes.

Investment Masters Class. n.d. "Efficient Markets." Retrieved September 20, 2022. http://mastersinvest.com/efficientmarketsquotes.

Investment Masters Class. n.d. "Moats." Retrieved September 18, 2022. http://mastersinvest.com/moats.

Klarman, S. A. 1991. *Margin of Safety: Risk-Averse Value Investing Strategies for the Thoughtful Investor*. HarperBusiness.

Klarman, S. 2008. "Preface." *Security Analysis* by Benjamin Graham.

Lynch, P. & Rothchild, J. 1995. *Learn to Earn: A Beginners Guide to the Basics of Investing and Business*. Simon & Schuster.

Lynch, P., and Rothchild, J. 2000. *One Up on Wall Street*. Simon & Schuster.

MacroTrends. n.d. "Gold prices—100-year historical chart." Retrieved September 17, 2022. https://www.macrotrends.net/1333/historical-gold-prices-100-year-chart.

Markopolos, H. 2011. *Harry Markopolos: "How to spot a fraud."* Bloomberg.com. September 23. Retrieved September 18, 2022. https://www.bloomberg.com/news/articles/2011-09-22/harry-markopolos-how-to-spot-a-fraud.

Marks, H. 2004. The Happy Medium. Oaktree Capital Management. July 20. https://www.oaktreecapital.com/docs/default-source/memos/2004-07-21-the-happy-medium.pdf?sfvrsn=4bbc0f65_2.

Marks, H. 2008. The Limits of Negativism. Oaktree Capital Management. October 15. https://www.oaktreecapital.com/docs/default-source/memos/2008-10-15-the-limits-to-negativism.pdf?sfvrsn=fbbc0f65_2.

Marks, H. 2018. *Mastering the Market Cycle: Getting the Odds on Your Side.* Mariner Books.

Martin E. 2018. "Here's exactly what an index fund is—and why it's Warren Buffett's favorite way to invest." CNBC. April 24. https://www.cnbc.com/2018/04/24/why-an-index-fund-is-warren-buffetts-favorite-way-to-invest.ht.

Melloy, J. 2017. "Buffett slams Wall Street 'monkeys', says hedge funds, advisors have cost clients $100 billion." CNBC. Febuary 25. https://www.cnbc.com/2017/02/25/buffett-slams-wall-street-monkeys-says-hedge-funds-cost-100-billion.html.

Moyer, L. 2017. "Warren Buffett's Big Bank score proves his saying true once again: 'be greedy when others are fearful." CNBC. June 30. Retrieved September 15, 2022. https://www.cnbc.com/2017/06/30/buffetts-big-bank-score-proves-be-greedy-when-others-are-fearful.html.

Munger, Charlie. n.d. "The big money is not in the buying and selling, but in the waiting." Quotefancy. Retrieved September 14, 2022. https://quotefancy.com/quote/756828/Charlie-Munger-The-big-money-is-not-in-the-buying-and-selling-but-in-the-waiting.

Public Broadcasting Service. n.d. "Interview with Peter Lynch: Betting on the Market." *Frontline*. PBS. Retrieved September 18, 2022. https://www.pbs.org/wgbh/pages/frontline/shows/betting/pros/lynch.html.

Public Broadcasting Service. n.d. "The Panic of 1873." PBS. Retrieved September 14, 2022. https://www.pbs.org/wgbh/americanexperience/features/grant-panic.

Staff, T. S. 2022. "What was the dot-com bubble & why did it burst?" TheStreet. May 31. Retrieved September 15, 2022. https://www.thestreet.com/dictionary/d/dot-com-bubble-and-burst.

Stern School of Business, New York University. n.d. "Historical Returns on Stocks, Bonds, and Bills: 1928–2021." Retrieved September 17, 2022. https://pages.stern.nyu.edu/~adamodar/New_Home_Page/datafile/histretSP.html.

Szramiak, J. n.d. "Here's How Warren Buffett Views Risk." Business Insider. May 31. Retrieved September 20, 2022. https://www.businessinsider.com/heres-how-warren-buffett-views-risk-2016-3.

Thiel, P., and Masters, B. 2015. *Zero to One: Notes on Startups or How to Build the Future*." Virgin Books.

US Department of the Treasury. 2022. "Financial Panic of 1873." February 11. Retrieved September 14, 2022. https://home.treasury.gov/about/history/freedmans-bank-building/financial-panic-of-1873.

Vintage Value Investing. 2015. "Charlie Munger interview with the BBC (2012) [10:56]." Harvest. December 18. Retrieved September 20, 2022. https://www.hvst.com/posts/charlie-munger-interview-with-the-bbc-2012-10-56-wLmTDNzz.

Wathen, J. 2017. "1 Stock That Was Pivotal in Billionaire Warren Buffett's Career." The Motley Fool. May 27. Retrieved September 16, 2022. https://www.fool.com/investing/2017/05/27/1-stock-that-was-pivotal-in-billionaire-warren-buf.aspx.

Yahoo! 2021. "Warren Buffett: 3 to 6 stocks is enough." Retrieved September 16, 2022. https://www.yahoo.com/lifestyle/warren-buffett-3-6-stocks-131512554.html.

ABOUT THE AUTHOR

Ashray Jha went through a remarkable life journey before he could write his first book. Growing up, he had an active lifestyle, playing basketball, soccer, going swimming, and he pursued a black belt in karate. Unfortunately, at the age of ten, Ashray was diagnosed with a benign brain tumor located in the cerebellum. After the surgery, his balance and coordination were severely affected. Going through this ordeal and not being able to do any activity that he could do before was mentally and emotionally difficult. Ashray had to work day and night just to regain strength in his muscles, speech, and fine motor skills. The everyday activities of life were a struggle. He felt hopeless at times, thinking it would be easier to just give up on ever achieving his dreams. Ashray faced a lot of adversity and judgments from some on what he could or could not do based on his appearance and disability. This made him feel that he would never be successful. Undeterred, Ashray went through countless hours of physical, speech, and occupational therapy to regain some functions and now lives an independent life.

While going through this major challenge, Ashray found his passion in investing and analyzing the competitive business landscape. Going through his investing journey, he realized that the same dedication and motivation needed for achieving his life goals were also needed to achieve his financial goals. Not only does he want to simplify the complex world of investing, but he also wants to serve as an example for anyone who may be facing obstacles or challenges in life that no matter what situation you are in, do not let anyone tell you that you cannot achieve your personal or financial goals in life.

Printed in the USA
CPSIA information can be obtained
at www.ICGtesting.com
LVHW091206150524
780221LV00002B/207